Hiding Paradise

Puzzling Through Romance Series

Miranda Herald

My Koala Pouch

Contents

Also By Miranda Herald

Loves Cats Series:

Prequel Chapters: Willa's Blooper Reel- FREE at www.mirandaherald.com

Book 1: Loves Cats, Anonymous

Book 2: Swipe Right for More Cats

Book 3: Free Shipping with More Cats

Puzzling through Romance Series:

Prequel Novella: Blundering through Paradise- FREE at www.mirandaherald.com

Book 1: Outwitting Paradise

Book 2: Misplacing Paradise

Book 3: Hiding Paradise

Book 4: Delivering Paradise

Smitten Scientists

Book 1: Catch and Release

Book 2: The Turtle and the Hare

Book 3: Wild Goose Chase

Chapter 1

Woman Overboard

Gina

Gina looked wide-eyed at the destruction all around her. *This is the paradise I chose as my refuge? What was I thinking?*

She took a deep breath, squared her shoulders, and turned around to the driver of the boat that gave her a ride. "Thank you so much for bringing me out here. The dock looks like the storm hit it pretty badly, but it's getting shallow. If you can just get me as close to shore as is safe, I will climb down the ladder on the side of your boat and walk to shore through the shallows."

The kindly older man, Chester, who was the captain of the small ocean vessel she'd rented, furrowed his bushy eyebrows. "Miss, I'm having second thoughts. I agreed to drive you out here, but I can't, in good conscience, leave you here. Hurricane Karen wrecked this island, and if you get off this boat, you will strand yourself. Listen, I know you really wanted to take a trip out here, but that island isn't safe. I'm going to take this boat back to the mainland, and I'll give you a refund. I'm retired and don't truly need the income. Besides, a few hundred dollars isn't worth your life."

Gina panicked. "I can't go back. I have to get on this island. Today is my first day of work as the island's chef."

Chester gently shook his graying head. "I'm sorry, miss. There isn't anyone here. Whoever you were supposed to work for probably evacuated for the hurricane like everyone else."

I can't go back to that life. I have to make this new life work, no matter what. Out of desperation more than determination, she swung a small backpack onto her back, containing all of her life's possessions. She secured the ponytail holding back her thick brown hair, took off her sunglasses, and cradled them in her right hand. She ungracefully dove her slim body off the side of the boat straight into the clear, sparkling water. She started swimming to shore.

Chester yelled from his boat. "Wait, miss! Where are you going? There are rumors about that island. I never gave them any credence until now. That isn't the kind of place I want to drop anyone off. Please come back. I'll take you anywhere else you want to go."

Gina walked up onto shore, dripping wet. She slid her glasses back on and turned around to wave at Chester. "Thank you again for bringing me to Riley's Paradise Island. I have it from here."

Gina thought she heard him say something about crazy women but couldn't be sure over the waves gently rushing onto the shore. She turned around and walked into the jungle along the largest path she could find leading away from the docks. *I need to dry out my bag soon. I only have two changes of clothing, my last forty dollars, and a hairbrush they gave me at the shelter.*

Tree limbs covered the path and plants were already growing upright in the middle of the walkway, showing that no one had cared for it in a while. *What have I gotten myself into? Maybe Chester was right, I should have gone back with him. If I had anywhere else to go, I would have.*

Despite the chaos, the jungle was full of life. Monkeys chattered as they swung through the trees. Birds sang as they flew through the canopy. Insects buzzed as they went about their business of pollinating the plentiful flowers lining her path. There was a beauty to the surrounding disorder that was breathtaking. She had seen nothing quite like it before in her life.

At one point, Gina caught her foot in a simple slipknot animal trap. *Odd that it would be right along a main walking path. Whoever set it must not know much about trapping.* She didn't know a ton, but it looked set way too big to catch any local wild game. Gina didn't think too much of it as she loosened the loop around her foot and reset the trap with a smaller loop as best as she could off the path.

A large tree with a structure attached like a treehouse had fallen across her path. She spotted a can of food lying on the ground and picked it up. She added it to her pack, not sure how she would get it open.

After several hours of circumventing obstacles, she came upon a large Mexican-style hacienda. It was brown with green trim and looked like they'd built it to blend in with the surrounding jungle. A large tree had fallen on the house and crumpled a part of the roof. *Looks like I found the owner's house. I hope they aren't mad that I'm late. It took me longer to navigate this island than I planned. I was supposed to be at work by nine a.m. today, and it's already closer to noon.*

She took the comb out of her pack and brushed her hair before putting it back into the ponytail. She tried to smooth out her mostly dried clothing, took off her sunglasses, and stashed them in her pack. *I wish I had something nicer to wear for my first day of work. I probably look like something the tide brought in.*

She made her way to the main entrance. There were two metal lattice doors, one behind the other, that looked like they led into a courtyard of some type. They reminded her of the portcullis gates of a castle.

To the left of the door, there was a keypad. She tried activating it by touching it, making sure it turned on, but it didn't respond at all. *Great, it's not working. I wonder what else the storm damaged. Hopefully, the kitchen is still serviceable.*

Gina called out through the gate. "Hello! Is someone there? It's me, Gina. I'm here to start work as your chef." No one answered. Dread filled Gina's stomach. No one was waiting for her.

What if Chester was right? What if they have evacuated the island? Come to think of it, they would have had no way of alerting me if they left. As soon as I secured this job, I left home and didn't leave a forwarding number. What have I gotten myself into?

Gina opened her backpack and lay the contents out in the sun to dry. They already smelled musty from being in her pack for so long. She secured the forty dollars under a rock. A lot of good that would do her out in the middle of the jungle.

She made her way back through the forest until she came to the treehouse. *I found a can of food here. Maybe more supplies fell out when this tree crashed. Although, why someone would live in a treehouse when there is a giant house nearby, I can't guess.*

After searching for a few hours, she found a can opener and a knife. There was a metal net attached to the bottom of the treehouse, but she couldn't get it free and didn't know what she would do with it if she did. She was hoping to find more, but at least she could have a meal before she figured out what to do tomorrow.

Gina used the can opener to open the can of chicken noodle soup. She slurped it down cold from the can. *I'm still starving. It has to be close to dinner time by now.* What should I do for the night? Gina climbed through the window of the treehouse, lying on the ground. A monkey yelled at her as it scampered out the other window.

She stood up on one wall that was now a floor. It was slightly crumpled where it fell but was otherwise intact. A broken table lay in the corner of the room. *Well, I guess this is better than sleeping out in the open.*

Gina left to gather her things that were now dry. To her horror and dismay, the forty dollars was gone.

Chapter 2

Amazonian Warrior

G ina

Gina sat on the floor that had once been a wall in the darkness. Only the moon shining through the trees provided a little light to see by. She listened to the eerie sounds of insects, monkeys, and who knew what else all around her. In the daylight, the aftermath of the storm was ironically beautiful and inspiring. At night, it felt like she was in the middle of a horror movie, about to be eaten at any moment.

Gina berated herself. *I should have stayed home. What was I thinking coming out here? How naïve I was to think I could start over. Now, I'm stranded on a broken-down deserted island with nothing to eat and drink. I even lost the last bit of money to my name. Thieving monkeys.*

Something was moving outside of the treehouse. She hugged her knees to herself and stayed stock still until the noises passed.

She spoke out loud to ease her fears. "What am I afraid of? That there's a dinosaur out there that hunts by movement? Although, since I know I won't get sleep anyway, I should probably think of a plan for tomorrow."

Grabbing her backpack, she unzipped it, unpacked it, and set the contents on the floor in front of her. "First thing is inventory. I have a knife, backpack, can opener, empty can, and two changes of clothing. For housing, I have a mostly intact downed treehouse. For food and water, I have nothing. I guess that's the plan for tomorrow. Food and water."

She neatly packed the soft clothing back into her pack but left out the metal items. "Hopefully, my new employers will be back soon. If not, I guess I have no choice but to make the best of things. I can't leave this island even if I want to."

After a few minutes of quiet, she softly admitted the truth to herself. "Honestly, I don't think I would leave even if I could. I know I was having a pity party a bit ago, but being a hermit, surviving off the land, is so much better than going home. At least I can be myself here."

A daydream ran through Gina's head where she spent the next several years alone on the island. Her hair was dirty and overgrown, and she drew a face on a coconut and spoke to it as her only friend...

Coconuts! Surely there will be some on this island. They're all around this area on the mainland. I'll walk to the shore. If I can find a coconut tree, then I will have all the sustenance I need.

Feeling better, Gina lay down on the floor. She placed her backpack full of clothing under her head and laid the knife down right beside her. Eventually, she fell asleep, exhausted from the mental and physical strain of the past year. She was finally free.

***

Gina woke early the next morning to a fly landing on her face. She swatted it away and sat up. Daylight streamed through the window above her and through a few areas where the boards were loose from the fall.

She grinned as she stood up and stretched. *Today is the first day of the rest of my life. It feels so good. I will never let another man get close to me again. I'm done with them. I'm much better off on my own.*

Wistful images of a cottage by the seashore and a mysterious stranger passed through her mind. She forcefully pushed the thoughts away. *That may have been the life I once wanted, but it is not the life for me. I've learned the hard way that I can only depend on myself.*

After packing up the rest of her supplies into her backpack, Gina made her way back out to the beach. On the path, she passed the slipknot that had caught her the day before. Now, there was a small rabbit panicking as it struggled to get loose.

Gina swung her backpack around and pulled out the large knife. She looked at the knife and looked at the rabbit. She knelt in front of it and spoke apologetically. "I'm sorry, little one, but this is a matter of survival."

The rabbit struggled even harder at the sound of her voice, its large innocent black eyes looking for an escape. "I know how it feels to be trapped. To feel like there is no escape."

With tears in her eyes, she loosened the noose around the rabbit's foot. Immediately, he darted off into the brush and disappeared. *Well, there goes the meal I needed to survive. I hope I don't regret that later.* It was probably for the best. She didn't have a fire or know how to clean a rabbit anyway. Gina reset the trap, just in case.

Maybe she would do better with a coconut. At least that couldn't look at her mournfully as she was about to eat it. She chuckled to herself. *That is, if I don't draw eyes on it first.*

Feeling more confident, she repeated a mantra. "I will find a coconut tree. I will find a coconut tree. I will find a coconut tree." A simple mantra like that was the only way she could break free from the emotional manipulation and fear that had held her captive for so long.

She laughed as she spoke aloud. This was the most carefree she had felt in so long. "Who cares if the monkeys think I'm crazy? Maybe I am."

On the beach, she found lots of interesting things that had washed to shore during the storm. There were creatures like jellyfish, starfish, and the mermaid purses that held young stingrays. She found an intact empty conch shell, so she placed it in her backpack.

There was lots of wood and branches along the shore. At one point, she found a metal pole sticking into the sand. She pulled it out and dropped it in surprise when she realized one end of it was sharp, like a spear or a javelin. She carried it along with her. *I feel like a real warrior woman now. Maybe I will start a new colony of Amazonian warriors right here.*

She imagined an abandoned infant girl washing up on shore in a small, oar-less rowboat. She would name the girl and care for her like her own, teaching her to hunt and gather food from the surrounding jungles. *I guess I should probably be able to find food on this island or dispatch a rabbit before that daydream comes true. Oh well, I'm never going to have a family anyway. Families are for people with less baggage.*

Gina walked on until she found a coconut tree in the distance. Elation spurred her to run ahead. She slowed down when she noticed several more of the metal spears scattered about the sand. Some lay flat, and the storm had partially buried some in the sand with points dangerously sticking up.

When she reached the tree, her heart dropped. All the coconuts were gone. *The storm must have knocked them off. What am I going to do now?* She walked around, trying to spy one lying on the ground.

She spotted a small green one and curled her lip in disgust. This one wasn't ripe yet. It would be mush inside.

She stuck it in her backpack, which was now comfortably full. With a spear in one hand, she continued to search around the base of the tree for any more loose coconuts. Suddenly, she heard a deep-throated growl behind her.

She spun around in shock to see a humongous, muscular tan dog with a black muzzle. The dog growled menacingly as it paced around Gina, staying out of reach of the spear. *Great, I landed on an island of wild dogs.* This was going to make her new hermit lifestyle a little more difficult.

Gina shook with fear as she tried to make her voice sound cheerful. "Hey, doggie. There's no need to be like that. I like dogs, really. I always wanted to have one of my own someday. Why can't we be friends?"

The dog snarled so loudly that spittle dripped from its mouth. Its legs tensed like it might jump. Gina cringed as she waved the spear, trying to scare it away. Instead of being intimidated, the dog barked loudly and growled ferociously as its ears lay flat against its head. She tried to step to the side, but the dog lunged, keeping her in place.

Chapter 3

Five-Star Accommodations

Gina

A large, muscular man burst through the brush. He had shaggy, dirty-blond hair and a goatee. He looked like he was in his early thirties, and he wore jeans and a camo shirt. Both Gina and the dog paused and stared at him, waiting to see what he would do.

Hmm... I have seen some people who match their dogs, but never this closely. They both have the same oversized body structure and matching fur/hair. He isn't the owner of this island, Nathan. I met him at my interview. Maybe I'm not the only squatter here. The question is, friend or foe?

The man spoke in a low, gruff voice. "Suzie, who do you have there?" He looked Gina over. Despite the spear, he called to Suzie, "Heel."

Immediately, the giant dog docilely walked over to the man and sat on her haunches beside him. The man patted the dog encouragingly without taking his eyes off Gina. "Ma'am, this is private property. I will escort you to your boat, where you can promptly return to the mainland."

Gina stood with her spear still pointed toward the man.

He looked at her quizzically. "Ma'am, you will not try to fight me, will you? Like a squirrel to a nut, I swear this island attracts the kookiest of folks. Let me warn you that a slim thing like you doesn't stand a chance against my years of hand-to-hand combat training in the military."

Gina mumbled, "Actually, I work here. Yesterday was my first day."

The man raised his eyebrows. "Nice try, but I know for a fact the island was empty until today when I arrived. Don't think that you can take advantage of the storm to steal things."

Gina's mouth dropped, and her hand tightened around the spear. "I stole nothing! All I have is my clothing... and I guess I found a knife, can opener, and a can of soup, but they were just lying around on the jungle floor. I ate the soup, but I will gladly pay for that after my new employer gives me my first paycheck."

Taking an enormous sigh, the man raised an eyebrow, frowned, and cocked his head. He didn't believe her. "Ma'am, my name is Dugan. I am the head of security at Riley's Paradise Island. I called all the new employees starting and pushed back their start date indefinitely once we found out this rabid wolf of a hurricane was coming through. There was only one employee I wasn't able to get a hold of." Examining her closely, Dugan looked her up and down. "I find it hard to believe that anyone in their right mind would stay on this island after they saw what a wreck it is right now. What's your name and where did you park your boat? I didn't see it near the docks when I arrived this morning."

Gina kept her eyes on Dugan but couldn't look him in the eye as she responded. "My name is Gina. Actually, I interviewed with my full name, Regina. Nathan Riley hired me a few months ago to be his new chef on this island." She watched as Dugan's eyes grew wide. "I don't have a boat. I jumped off the boat that brought me here because he didn't want to let me off."

Dugan stared at her in silence for a few minutes before answering. "Well, I'll be a beaver busy with his dam. That's the best work ethic

I've ever heard of." He raised his hands and calmly approached her like someone used to taming scared animals. "You can put down the spear, Gina. A woman named Regina was the person I couldn't get a hold of. I'm sorry I didn't believe you. Would you like to come with me to take inventory of the island? I'm taking some pictures to send to Nathan."

Gina nodded. She lowered the spear but carried it with her. "I guess I can't blame you since I'm dressed in these dirty, wrinkly clothes. It's just been a rougher first day on the job than I expected."

Dugan shook his head as she followed him and Suzie down an overgrown path back into the jungle. "Unfortunately, from what I've seen so far, it isn't going to be safe for Nathan's family to return for a while. I have a lot of work to do cleaning up this island and making it safe." He pointed to the setting sun. "It's too late to take you back tonight, so I can set you up in a spare room in Nathan's house. Then, tomorrow morning, I'll take you back to the mainland. I'll be in touch in another month or two when we get the employee housing built and it's safe for Nathan and his family to return."

Panic raced through Gina. She couldn't go back. This was supposed to be her refuge. If she left, where would she go for two months that would be safe? She no longer had even a dollar to her name.

Dugan shot out his arm and stopped her short of walking into a net that was made of some kind of clear plastic, hanging from a tree. It was almost impossible to see unless you knew it was there. *How odd.* The storm had blown things around, making it look like the island was booby-trapped.

During their walk, she began using her spear as a walking stick. More than once she caught it in an animal trap or it detected a sink-hole. For what was once a beautiful paradise island, it was sure full of surprises.

They walked along in silence for a while, working their way over and around obstacles. Dugan didn't seem like a man of many words, but that was all right. Neither was she. Finally, he broke the silence. "You said that you arrived last night. Where did you sleep? Do you have a tent set up somewhere? Where are the rest of your things?"

Gina looked down at her feet, ashamed of how little she had. When she was younger, she'd expected she would own her own house by this age. It would shock her younger self to see her now. *If I'd tried to take more, he would have noticed what I was planning. All I could take with me was what looked like a normal trip to my fitness class.*

Tentatively, Gina answered, "I have nothing else. Just what's in my backpack. I slept in a treehouse that fell over from the storm."

Dugan didn't probe any deeper. He just grumbled something about an employee-of-the-month award, and Gina rolled her eyes. They could post her picture up for all the monkeys to see.

Shaking his head, Dugan turned, as if checking on her. "Yes, I noticed that the treehouse fell this morning when I started taking pictures of the destruction. Like a buzzard mourning a good meal, Nathan won't be too pleased. That treehouse was a joy from his childhood that he built with his brother. At least my cottage came out of it mostly unscathed. We will have to see how Nathan's compound and Mr. Walter Riley's mansion made it through this mess."

Before long, they came upon the large hacienda that Gina had found earlier where she lost her forty dollars. The sun hung low in the sky, and the shadows of the trees stretched eerily across the building.

Dugan stopped and snapped a few pictures with his phone. He walked around to get a few different angles. Suzie walked around beside him, sniffing and ignoring Gina. "That tree would have caused some damage to some of the extra bedrooms on the upper floor, but luckily, Ms. Brianna won't be sleeping there anymore. There are a few windows out near the kitchen with some debris inside, but honestly, it could've been a lot worse. Let's head inside and see if there is more damage that we can't see from the outside."

Gina silently followed Dugan up to the front gate of Nathan's compound. He put his eye up to a retinal scanner. He blinked his eyes in an odd pattern. When nothing happened, he tapped the machine and opened an electrical panel behind it. Gina waited patiently. No luck.

Dugan turned toward Gina. "I'm sorry, Gina. It looks like the electricity is down. We can't get into Nathan's compound until I get the security of this place up and running. You will have to spend the night with me back at my cottage. I'll give you the bed, and I'll sleep by the hearth with Suzie."

Gina shook her head. She would not move in with another man who would dictate her every move. "I appreciate the offer, but no thank you. I found my own accommodations." She turned and, without another word, walked back to the broken-down treehouse.

Chapter 4

Fire!

Gina

Dugan watched Gina disappearing through the trees. "You're like a racehorse on the track. Wait! Where are you going?" He chased after her. "It's getting dark soon, and it's not safe out here at night with these obstacles obstructing the paths. The storm barely touched my cottage, but it's in the other direction."

Gina held back tears. "I will not stay in your cottage, and it's not your job to keep me safe." She waved the spear around in a dramatic but non-threatening manner. She heard Suzie growl a warning, regardless.

"I can take care of myself. I'm going back to the downed treehouse. I came here for a job, and I don't intend to leave unless Nathan fires me." Gina forcefully walked on, not really paying attention to her feet anymore.

She barely made it another yard. "Ahhh!" She shrieked as her foot caught on a large animal snare. Her spear went flying from her hands as she flew forward. Her forehead banged off a log, and she fell face-first into a muddy section of the path.

Suzie got to her first and licked her ear, as if concerned. Gina groaned as she swatted the large dog away. Dugan was there only a few moments later. He picked her up off the ground like she was as light as a feather and set her back on her feet.

He stood close as he examined her head wound, muttering to himself. "I think I now understand why a male grizzly lives alone. Who knows the whims of women?"

Gina tried to brush as much of the mud off of herself as possible. She felt cared for by this large protective man but pushed those warm, fuzzy feelings away. He was a little too close. *I'm never going to let myself make that mistake again.*

Gina tried to take a step backward, but her trapped foot wouldn't let her. It was sore. "I'm fine, just a little muddy. I'll be on my way. I'll start working on cleaning up this island tomorrow to earn my keep."

Dugan frowned and stepped close to look into her eyes. "Well then, we are at an impasse. I can't possibly leave you by yourself now that you have a head wound. It doesn't look like you have a concussion, but I should still keep an eye on the island's new prize employee just in case."

Dugan knelt down in the mud and gently released her foot from the trap. "Listen, this storm set us back a few months. I will make sure that Nathan understands what a great work ethic you have, but please just go home for a few months. It's not safe here right now. Unlike a lion stalking his prey, I can't monitor you all the time out here. I have a lot to get cleaned up and safe before the Rileys come home. I promise I'll call you when we're ready for you."

Gina gingerly moved her newly released foot. *Where in the world can I spend the next few months until they are ready for me? I can't tell him I have no home and not a penny to my name. That would make me sound desperate. This is supposed to be my refuge. I can't let this funny-speaking oversized teddy bear take that away from me.*

Gina had to stay strong. She couldn't risk him making her leave. "You said yourself that you have a ton of work to do before the Rileys return. Besides my cooking, I have some basic handyman skills and can wield a scrub brush much better than my lost spear. I can get the house all back in tip-top shape while you work out here. That way, you don't have to feel responsible for me and I can help you with all of this mess."

Gina turned and hobbled around as she searched the overgrown jungle brush for her metal spear. "Aha! Found it!" She picked it up. "In the meantime, I am living on my own and will not be coming back to your cabin. I *can* take care of myself."

She turned her back to Dugan before he could respond. Limping, she held her head high as she tried her best to march the last of the way to the treehouse in the dusk. She was proud that she had stuck up for herself. Memories from earlier flooded her as her feelings of triumph strengthened her to remain independent and free. She wouldn't let any man take that away from her again.

Although, I am a bit surprised Dugan let me walk away. Once Maxwell decided she was going to do something, he never let her wiggle out of it. He always needed to know exactly where she was and what she was doing. What kind of man was Dugan?

Her stomach growled. She pulled the large knife and the mostly green coconut out of her pack. It took a while, but eventually, she managed to dehusk it. The shell was incredibly hard, but after she hit it with a rock near the little circles that looked like eyes, she could crack it open. *Sorry, my first island friend.*

The inside of the mostly green coconut was not the sweet, firm flesh of a ripe coconut. Instead, it was slightly jelly-like with a lot of coconut water in the center. Gina grimaced as she drank the water, but her taste buds were pleasantly surprised at the slightly sweet taste. She scooped a handful of the gooey flesh out and ate. *This texture is horrible, but at least the taste isn't too bad, and it will allow me to survive. So far, this paradise hasn't turned out to be much of a refuge like I was hoping.*

After she finished her meal, Gina's stomach still grumbled, but she took her meager supplies and climbed through the window to enter the treehouse. She sat in the growing darkness, waiting out the night. Eventually, she laid the knife down beside her and plumped up her backpack to make a pillow like she had the previous night. She lay there in silence, waiting for sleep to come.

Curiously, she heard a large animal loudly sniffing and moving through the brush all around the base of the treehouse. *Is that Suzie or some other large animal?* Didn't Dugan say something about it being dangerous out there at night?

Then she heard another sound, like something or some things running around outside like crazy. Gina got up and tried to peek through the window to see what could be out there. *I hope a pack of wild animals can't make it inside through the crunched-in end of the treehouse.*

A monkey darted around the window she was peering out, scaring her half to death. It screeched loudly as it disappeared back into the dark forest. Then Gina smelled smoke. A lot of smoke. She spotted a flicker of a flame only about twenty-five feet from her location, but it was impossible to make anything else out between the pitch-black night and the thick gray smoke filling the air all around her.

I'm trapped. There's a jungle fire out there. If I try to get out, jungle creatures might get me. If I stay here, I might burn alive. Gina threw her pack over her shoulder and grabbed her spear. She would face whatever was out there. She would not cower in fear ever again.

Chapter 5

Campout

Gina

Gina slowly eased open the window and crawled out, spear first. She stood up and tried to locate danger in the darkness. She tried to orient herself to where the fire was coming from so she could make a run for it.

What she wasn't ready for was for her ankles to be attacked. A two-foot-high puppy darted out of the forest, sniffing her ankles and licking her excitedly. He was tan, similar to Suzie, but had a few more black splotches on his coat.

Dugan walked around from the other side of the treehouse. "Pongo! Down, boy!" The puppy ignored him. Dugan walked over and took a firm but gentle hand to push the wiggling puppy to a sitting position on the ground. He repeated himself. "Down, boy."

Gina did a double take. *Am I seeing things? Is that a small monkey sitting on Dugan's shoulder, holding onto his ear with its little hands? Who is this man? Does he think he's the beast master or something?*

Dugan released the puppy, and the dog sped off down a path as fast as his little legs could take him, jumping over logs on the way. At some point, he must have turned around because a few moments later, Gina spotted the active puppy running down the path in the other direction. Never straying too far out of sight.

Dugan looked at her apologetically. "Sorry about Pongo. He has a long way to go with his training, but he's sharp, so I will have him well-trained and polite like Suzie soon. If you would like to join me around the other side of the treehouse, I made a fire. It's smoky from the wet wood I had to use, but I brought you some dinner and fresh water."

It touched Gina's heart that he would figure out how to do something nice for her without stifling her independence. "Thank you. You didn't have to do this. You know I was doing fine on my own, right?"

Dugan held up his hands in mock surrender. "Like a dolphin in the water, you looked like you were getting along perfectly before I even came back here. Unfortunately, I get lonely sometimes and would appreciate the company over dinner. Would you mind humoring me? Please?"

Gina gave him a sideways glance, but at that moment her stomach growled loudly, making Dugan smile. *It's hard to say I'm not hungry and don't need his food when my stomach is betraying me. I feel like I could eat a horse and drink a river right now. Uh-oh. This man's peculiar way of talking is rubbing off on me.*

Begrudgingly, she nodded. "Maybe I'll have a little something to munch on."

She followed Dugan around the edge of the treehouse. He had set up a small camp in a clearing about twenty-five feet away. There were two cots set up on opposite sides of the fire with blankets. Suzie lay in front of a large fire, giving her puppy an exasperated look as he ran back and forth with excitement.

Dugan walked over to the tripod he had over the top of the fire. He used a soup spoon and stirred something in a large cast-iron pot. He pointed to one cot. "I just got this cooking, so it's going to be a while.

Help yourself to a cot and take a seat. I brought you one in case you wanted to take it into the treehouse with you."

Gina looked down at herself. Mud, bug bites, and other unidentifiable debris covered her body. "That's very thoughtful, but it's been a rough last two days. I'm a mess. I don't think those blankets would survive me."

Dugan smiled at her reassuringly. "Like a raccoon softening its food, they will wash. Don't worry, I've seen worse when I had to spend two weeks hiding in a jungle of South America doing surveillance work. I can't say those days with the military were my best memories, but I survived and so did my blanket."

They sat in silence for a while. Pongo came over and fell asleep at her feet. Suzie lay comfortably, warming herself by the fire, and the monkey occasionally chattered and picked something out of Dugan's hair.

I feel like I'm in a story with Tarzan. Just call me Jane.

Eventually, the stew was ready. They talked little, but that was okay. Gina was enjoying the warmth, safety, and camaraderie around the fire. She never took her cot into the treehouse. With a full tummy, she felt too safe and comfortable right where she was to move. Dugan threw more wood on the fire as she curled up and drifted off to sleep.

***

The next morning, Gina woke abruptly, sitting up. The small monkey that had stayed with Dugan last night scampered off of her blanket, chattering angrily at being disturbed. It took a few moments for her to take in her surroundings through her blurry, sleepy eyes.

The deep voice of Dugan drew her attention. Suzie lay by the fire, eating her breakfast. "I see you met Chee Chee. That's Brianna's pet. Brianna is Nathan's wife. I'm watching him while they are on their honeymoon at a castle in Scotland."

Gina nodded her head. "Yeah, I noticed him last night. I thought you looked a lot like Tarzan with a monkey on your shoulder, feeding him bits of food."

Dugan gave the monkey a fake glare. "You know how I told you that the hurricane left my cottage mostly untouched? Well, after leaving Chee Chee and Pongo in there for a few hours yesterday while I assessed the safety of the island, my place looked like its own hurricane had hit it hard."

Dugan looked at her curiously as he handed her a protein bar and passed her a water bottle with a filter spout on the top that looked freshly filled. "I was wondering if you would ask about the monkey last night. You never did."

Gina smiled. "I was enjoying the crackle of the fire and the sounds of the surrounding jungle. It was very soothing."

Dugan's bushy eyebrows rose in surprise. "Most people I meet can't stand silence. The sounds of the jungle make them jumpy, like a rabbit being chased by a fox. Listen, if you truly are determined to stay here, we can go with your plan."

Gina stopped crunching on her protein bar in shock. She looked at him warily. *When are the manipulations going to come? Maybe he's even craftier than Maxwell. Everyone thought he was so charming. I didn't realize what I had gotten myself into until it was too late.*

Dugan continued talking, seemingly unaware of her distrustful glances. "Today, I need to head over to the other side of the island and take some pictures of Mr. Walter Riley's mansion so I can send a full damage report to Nathan. Walter is Nathan's father, by the way. I'm sure you will get to know the whole quirky family well when they come home." He grimaced and took a swig of water. "Although, I'm not looking forward to giving Nathan a status report of this island. There is a lot of work to do to make it safe and habitable again." He set the water bottle back down as he continued. "After we check out Walter Riley's home and take some pictures, then I can go to the control room and hopefully figure out where the power outage is coming from. When I was there yesterday, everything looked in decent repair, so hopefully, it won't take too long to find what is causing the power outages." Chee Chee momentarily broke Dugan's thought process as he climbed onto the large man and sat upon his shoulder.

"If everything goes well, we will have you into Nathan's compound by nightfall. I'll help with some of the more minor repairs, and then I will leave you to the cleaning while I make the main paths safe. I have a construction crew on standby to build the employee housing, but they can help with any major household repairs first." Dugan looked down as Pongo came over to greet them. After he got a few reassuring pats, he raced back into the nearby brush to investigate.

Dugan's bright blue eyes softened his gruff exterior. "Would you like to go on a jungle adventure with me today?"

Chapter 6

Pongo to the Rescue?

G^{ina}

Following close behind Dugan, Gina watched as two beautiful blue parrots spooked from a nearby tree. She spotted a few flowers blossoming on vines that wrapped around a massive trunk. It was truly amazing how fast the local foliage was recovering from such a massive disaster. She doubted the people who lived on the mainland were having such luck.

"Like an eagle looking for a mouse, keep your eyes peeled. Usually, the traps and puzzles around here won't hurt you, but this hurricane messed them all up. Right now, this island isn't necessarily a safe place to traverse, and that's why my priority is safety before I invite any others back to the island." Dugan used a machete to hack through a path that had mostly grown over. Chee Chee sat on his shoulder, with one hand on his ear.

Gina gave him a bit of swinging distance as she continued safely behind him. Before they'd started on this adventure, Dugan had set her up with an extra water bottle and some bug spray. He was alarmed at the number of bug bites she had gotten, so he convinced her to borrow a long-sleeved shirt, even though it was so big on her she could have fit two of her inside. She pulled the excess fabric and tied it in a knot at her waist so she could navigate the jungle comfortably.

In his own backward way, Dugan was very thoughtful and sweet. He didn't even know Gina but had taken efforts above and beyond to make her comfortable, with no gain to himself.

I'm comfortable instead of upset that he interrupted my solitude, but I can't help feeling like the other shoe is going to drop. This is too good to be true, isn't it?

Suzie appeared out of some overgrowth and walked companionably beside Gina, wagging her massive tail as they walked. *Pongo seems to love everyone. I wonder how Dugan is going to train that crazy pup in island security?*

After a while, Dugan paused for a water break. Sweat covered his face and soaked through his shirt from hacking his way through the overgrown path, but he never complained. He also set out a small bowl of water for both dogs that they lapped up eagerly.

Curious, Gina asked him, "How did you get into training dogs for security?"

Dugan glanced fondly at Suzie. "In the military, they stationed me for about a year at a base whose focus was training dogs for various jobs, like security, bomb and drug identification, and a few other things. I helped while they stationed me there and thought the idea was brilliant. Using the keener senses of a canine and the intelligence of a human to make a powerful security team."

Dugan looked away. "Unfortunately, I found out the hard way that only half the team can be foiled way too easily. I'm lucky that Nathan is a kind enough man to give me another chance. He saw me as head of security when everyone else saw me as a broken man who couldn't handle society after leaving the military. For that, I will be forever grateful. I owe him everything."

Gina stared at Dugan, open-mouthed. *I can't believe he just told me something so personal about himself. He admitted mistakes and weaknesses. Maxwell would have blamed all of that on me. Maybe Dugan really is different.*

Dugan saw her staring then looked away and tucked his head. He picked up his machete and continued hacking away at the jungle even more vigorously than before.

Gina wanted to say something to reassure him he was doing a great job, that Nathan was right to see him as the capable head of security of this crazy island. That it was refreshing seeing a man who was so kind and real. Unfortunately, she didn't think he would hear over his chopping. Besides, the moment had passed.

Before long, Gina could see something bright red lying splintered against a tree. Dugan ignored it and kept making his way down the path. Gina stopped and examined what she could see from the path. Oddly enough, it looked almost like a bright red door splintered into a dozen different pieces. *It must have flown all the way out here from the house. Why else would a door be way out in the middle of nowhere?*

Gina took a step off the path toward the broken door. Immediately, her foot felt like a tight vise had grabbed it. It yanked her onto her back and dragged into the brush, Dugan none the wiser. Unable to scream, Gina used her arms to cover her face as sticks and twigs scratched at her face. Something dragged her about twenty feet off the path before she stopped.

Dazed, Gina's back ached horribly where it had hit plants and small rocks. She looked around to get her bearings and yelled out, "Dugan!" but was doubtful that he could hear her over his chopping. She was surrounded by thick, dense jungle except for the flattened path her body had just crashed through. *Dugan should be able to track me through that path, right? How long will it take him to take another water break and realize I'm gone?*

She examined her foot. The metal ring that caught it reminded her of a manacle. They'd attached it to a chain that ran underground where she could see a small slit surrounded by metal that the trap had pulled her along. It had trapped her foot near the path, and then some kind of machine underground had pulled her into the middle of nowhere.

What is this island? What practical use could this possibly have?

Pongo came through the brush, presumably investigating the noise. When he saw her, his entire backside wagged, and he started licking her face excitedly.

Gina covered her face with one of her hands. She pushed the puppy back a bit and petted his back. "Hello, Pongo. You're such a good boy for coming to find me. Can the good boy get Dugan?" Pongo tried to lick her face again. "No, no, buddy. I need you to get Dugan." She looked him in the eye and repeated, "Pongo, get Dugan. Go ahead, get Dugan."

The puppy barked excitedly and ran in circles around her like she was playing a game. Gina sighed and tried again. "Pongo, come here, boy." The puppy immediately came to Gina and lay down in front of her, even though he couldn't stop wiggling and wagging his tail.

Gina patiently tried again. "Pongo, go get Dugan. I need Dugan." Pongo barked loudly and ran around her again. Her shoulders slumped.

Gina spent the next few minutes fiddling with the manacle. She couldn't figure out a way to release it or get it off. She couldn't go anywhere, and her ankle was hurting severely.

Soon, she heard something large crashing through the brush toward her. Pongo barked even more excitedly. She called out, "Dugan! Dugan? Is that you?"

To Gina's relief, Dugan's gruff voice responded, "Gina, I'm almost to you. Are you all right?"

Before she could answer, Dugan burst past the last branches and leaves covering the path the trap dragged her down. Suzie was right on his heels. A look of concern crossed his face when he saw her. He immediately knelt on the ground and delicately examined her foot.

Gina said, "I'm stuck. I took a single step off the path and this manacle thing grabbed me and dragged me out here. Luckily, it didn't break my ankle, but it is very sore."

Dugan looked up and into her eyes. Their faces were inches from each other. Gina hadn't realized he was that close. To her surprise, Chee Chee jumped from Dugan's shoulder onto her own. The little monkey picked the sticks out of her hair and presumably looked for bugs.

Dugan chuckled at the monkey's antics. "You're right. It doesn't look like it's broken. The release for this trap is near the main path. I'll be right back." Dugan stood up and patted an excited Pongo. "Good boy. You found her, stayed with her, and alerted me to where she was. I was worrying the training wasn't sticking, but you are picking some things up after all."

He disappeared back down the path, and after a few moments, the manacle on her foot released. Gina immediately removed her foot and rubbed her ankle. It was red but not swollen.

Dugan came back down the path just as she was standing up and trying out her foot. With concern on his face, he asked, "Do you want to get on my back? I'll carry you to our impromptu camp at the fallen-down treehouse."

Gina laughed at him and realized it was the first time she had laughed in a long time. "I'm not a toddler in need of a piggyback ride!

Give me a few minutes to walk this off. I should be fine. It's feeling better already. What in the world was that thing, anyway?"

Dugan's face was a lot more emotive than she realized. She watched as he smiled at her laugh, then frowned at her response. "I don't want you pushing it. A sore ankle will only get worse if you try to do too much before it's ready." Dugan pointed to the trap. "As for the trap, the two brothers who live on this island are a little quirky. Nathan and Jackson grew up here alone as boys, and now they spend their time making traps to catch one another in. That's part of the reason I'm afraid to let anyone near the island right now. That hurricane disrupted a lot of them, and I don't know what they might do. Some of them could be very dangerous if they aren't working properly."

Dugan watched Gina move around more and more confidently. He gave Pongo another pat before the dog ran off into the woods, chasing something that moved fast. "I never said we work for normal folks, but they keep things interesting. Are you sure you're ready to continue? The mansion that Walter Riley, the owner of Riley's Paradise Island and his son, Jackson, live in is only about fifteen more minutes away."

Gina nodded and followed directly behind Dugan, not daring to take a step off the path. Chee Chee stayed with her for the time being. Intermittently, the little monkey would chatter as if having a conversation with her. His tiny fingers tickled as he held onto her ear like a handhold.

A short while later, they came across a gigantic mud pit. She cringed at the sight of it. *Ick.* Unlucky for the island owners, but lucky for her, a giant tower of some sort had fallen over from the storm and into the mud. It made a perfect pathway for Dugan, Gina, and the dogs to cross.

Gina's foot was getting really sore when they saw the trees thin out. She didn't dare tell Dugan about her pain for fear of being sent back.

She was about to suggest a brief break when they broke through the last trees.

She made a loud gasp of horror. Boards and stones lay haphazardly upon each other over the ruins of a house foundation. The storm had decimated the mansion.

Chapter 7

Minotaur Maze

D ugan "Gotcha! Like putting a diaper on a baby. A little fiddling and we are all set to go." Dugan looked behind him to where Gina was resting on a computer chair, drinking an iced tea and snacking on some chips they'd found in the kitchenette of the control room. She had a beautiful, heart-shaped face.

Dugan couldn't help his eyes wandering over her. She looked so tantalizing with his shirt hanging loosely over her slim form and a firm knot tightly around her waist. It stirred something deep inside of him he thought was long dead. *She is so out of my league. I need to let this one go.* His eyes stopped to see how she had her foot propped up on a second chair. *I think her ankle is bothering her more than she's letting on.*

Suzie lay at her feet, taking a nap after their long excursion to see the destruction of Walter and Jackson's mansion. *Even Suzie has taken a liking to that beautiful woman's calm demeanor. I've never seen her so comfortable around someone other than me before. Especially when that someone isn't feeding her.* He had left Pongo and Chee Chee back at his cottage before coming to the control room. Although he cringed at the mess those two would make, he thought it best not to attempt to fix electricity with a three-ring circus jumping around the room.

Dugan stood up and checked the computer monitors. He assessed their condition aloud, for Gina's sake. *I don't think I've talked this much in the whole last five years I've worked here.* "Let's see here. It looks like there is electricity running to most of Nathan's compound now. There's a direct line running underground to that building, so it wasn't harmed. Unfortunately, most of the rest of the island is going to be a work in progress until I find where the storm caused damage." Dugan turned to Gina. "All right, I think I've finished assessing the status of the island. Like a hippopotamus leaving the water, it's time for me to make the dreaded phone call updating Nathan. I might be on the phone for a while. Do you need anything first? Another drink or something else to eat?"

Gina smiled at him, and Dugan felt a joy deep in his chest, like he would do anything to see that smile again. *Oh, boy. I'm quite smitten. I will have to be careful so I don't make her feel uncomfortable. A beautiful woman like that obviously won't have the time of day for someone like me.*

Gina replied, "No, I'm still finishing this up. I'm good. I'm enjoying the rest right now because I'm sure as soon as we get into Nathan's compound, I will have my work cut out for me."

Dugan nodded and went into the kitchenette to make the call. He got out a notepad and pen to jot down any instructions Nathan had for him. He carefully looked through the photos he had taken over the past two days of the storm's carnage. As he sent the pictures to Nathan, he winced.

After I messed up with that smuggler who kidnapped Brianna, I have to prove that I can handle this. There is no way I can mess this up. I have to show Nathan he was right when he thought I was more than an ex-military officer struggling to find his way. I have to prove I can handle this job. Dugan dialed Nathan's number.

Nathan answered. "Hello? Dugan? I was glancing through those pictures you just sent me. They aren't pretty."

Dugan took a deep breath. "Sir, like a piano dropped from a three-story building, there was a lot of damage. There is only electricity running to the control room and a part of your compound. The rest of the island is down. A lot of your puzzles and traps are not working because of a lack of electricity or malfunctioning from damage from the storm. Your brother's house took some of the worst of the damage. Your treehouse didn't make it either."

Dugan heard sorrow in his boss's voice, but he was still all business as he responded. "How soon can we get the construction team out there? I know we originally planned for them to build the employee housing, but we can have them make repairs first. Don't have them worry about Dad and Jackson's house yet. That's going to be an extensive project all on its own. I'll talk to both of them about what they want to do with their house. Knowing Jackson, we will probably thrill him with the opportunity to build the mansion into a minotaur maze."

Dugan ignored Nathan's last comment. "Yes, sir. My plan is to get the island safe enough for them to get to work next week. In the meantime, I'm going to handle cleaning up the outside and fixing the rest of the electricity to the housing, and Gina will take care of fixing up the house."

Confused, Nathan replied, "Gina? Are you talking about the woman I hired to take over the cooking at the compound full-time?"

Dugan replied quickly. *I hope he isn't mad that I let her stay before the island is perfectly safe.* "Yes. Unfortunately, she was the only one of your new staff that I could not get a hold of to push back their start date. She showed up on her scheduled first day and has been adamant about getting right to work."

There was a long pause before Nathan answered. "All right, it sounds like she has a good work ethic. Just make sure she doesn't get caught in any of those misfiring traps you were talking about."

Nathan paused again, and Dugan could picture him running his hand through his hair as the man often did when stressed. Nathan took a deep breath before he continued talking. "After seeing those pictures, I think I'm going to extend our honeymoon until things are safe and back to working order. Hopefully, I can get a hold of my aunt to see about renting this castle longer, or maybe we will go visit her for a while. Do you think you can have my compound ready for us in six weeks?"

Dugan thought about the massive amount of destruction on the island. He wasn't the best at organizing people, and he knew it was going to be a humongous project, getting all the new employees trained and running efficiently. The construction workers weren't even on the island, much less building the employee housing yet. *I can't let Nathan down again.*

"Of course, sir. Like a bird returning to its nest, everything will be in order," Dugan promised, but his brow broke out into a sweat.

Chapter 8

Quirky Family

G ina

Gina hobbled behind Dugan as they checked the perimeter of Nathan's compound. She was doing her best to make sure that Dugan didn't notice her limp whenever he turned around. Suzie seemed to notice her distress and walked beside her closely. "Why did you pass up the main gate? It kind of reminds me of a castle door."

Dugan looked back at her and frowned. Gina wondered if he'd seen her favoring one leg, but no matter what he said, she would not let him give her a piggyback ride.

Dugan said, "Like any good soldier ant, I need to make sure the integrity of the walls is still good before we go inside. So far everything looks intact, even though we could see some roof damage from the front. They designed the gates after a double-gated castle portcullis. Any trespassers that don't know the correct passcode can get trapped between them."

Gina shivered and gave the gate a sideways glance. A sense of foreboding overcame her, and a flash of doubt. She chose a most peculiar place to build her new life. Were the Rileys mentally unstable or this suspicious for a reason? Was she in over her head?

They came upon an odd giant rectangular hole in the ground that covered the entire width of the path. Dugan looked at it, unsurprised, and walked through some brush to the side of the pathway.

Dugan commented to her over his shoulder as he walked, "Looks like the electricity isn't working for Nathan's trampoline trap. A slight inconvenience, but that doesn't have to be a priority to fix."

It didn't look like any kind of trampoline she had ever seen before. It seemed like there was mystery upon mystery on this island.

Giving the hole a wide berth, Gina asked, "Why are there traps all over this island? This seems excessive for two brothers playing practical jokes on each other. Are there some kind of wild animals on this island I need to be cautious of?"

"Suzie here is the only creature someone would need to worry about, but she knows you now, so you'll be fine. While it started with a young Nathan and Jackson trying to outwit each other, they have turned into more of a sophisticated security system. There have been problems with tourists trespassing, smugglers exchanging goods in the cove, and even poachers. These traps help deter unwanted visitors and immobilize them until I can remove them and make sure they don't come back."

Needing to make sure that she wasn't jumping from one unpleasant situation to another, Gina probed about the Rileys a little more. Dugan seemed loyal and indebted to the family, so she would have to be very careful about how she worded her questions not to offend him. Of course, the best way to learn about someone was through their stomach.

"In an effort to start meal planning for Nathan and the other Rileys, can you describe their preferences and temperaments to me? I don't suppose you know their favorite food, do you?"

Dugan paused and scratched his chin. "I'll try my best, but I don't see the family at a lot of mealtimes." He pointed at the building next to him. "So, you will primarily work here at the compound for Nathan. He likes meals that look fancier, but he also seems happy as a lark with something simpler. His daughter, Jenna, is rather hyper and sweet as a pea. She loves everything sugary and especially loves to help make chocolate chip cookies. Nathan's new wife, Brianna, seems to have some obsession with turkey sandwiches, but otherwise, she has seemed content to have both fancier meals with Nathan or animal crackers with Jenna."

Gina nodded her head. That didn't sound too bad. She had a handful of ideas going through her mind already of recipes that were not too demanding but looked impressive that might meet everyone's tastes. "What about the others? Didn't you say Nathan's dad and brother live on the island too?"

Pointing back into the lush jungle, Dugan answered while he slowly walked around the compound again. "Yes, we took pictures of their ruined house. I know Nathan didn't hire you to cook for them other than on special occasions, but that may have changed now that there is no other housing on the island. I can ask Nathan next time I talk to him if you want."

Gina stayed close enough to Dugan to talk while he continued his examinations. "Yes, thanks. That would help me a lot with planning future meals. What can you tell me about them?"

Dugan took a moment before answering. "Well, I have spent less time with Jackson and Walter than I have with Nathan, but I will tell you what I can. Like a peacock, Jackson loves a lot of flash and a lot of women but adores his niece, Jenna. Walter Riley still rules the family business, Riley's Games, with an iron fist and this island as well. He is grumpy and doesn't like to pass out compliments, but he also doesn't ask for a lot, either. Or at least he doesn't ask a lot from me."

Pursing his lips, Dugan added, "Although, like a gator that's spotted its next meal, I have seen a smile or two cross that crotchety old man's face lately. He's smitten with Debbie, the woman who used to cook and clean for all the Rileys on the island."

A loose root caught the front of Gina's shoe, causing her to trip. She reached out her hand to grab anything she could before falling, but immediately Dugan was there, holding her arm as she steadied herself. He didn't let go. "Thank you, Dugan. I should be fine now."

With a frown, Dugan let go of her arm but stayed close as he looked her over. "Are you sure you're all right? How is that ankle feeling? Like a flamingo, you're barely putting any weight on your other foot."

Gina shrugged. "I'm fine." As he watched her, she made care to put equal weight on each foot as she walked around him and continued their circuit around the building. She thought about everything Dugan had told her and decided quirky was probably the best way to describe this family. They were rich and had their own idiosyncrasies, but they didn't sound that bad and couldn't be to keep the respect of a man like Dugan.

She decided she needed to make things work here so she could uncover all the secrets of her refuge. Until she learned the ins and outs of this island, these puzzles and traps, Dugan would work to help keep her safe.

They walked farther and came across a giant pile of some type of slime. It covered the ground, trees, and nearby brush. A small rabbit wiggled around near the edge. The stuff covered his feet, and the poor little critter couldn't get out.

Gina asked, "What is that stuff?"

Dugan turned to her. "That's Nathan's mousetrap. Don't touch that slimy stuff. It's incredibly sticky, and it dries hard. Luckily, it's water-soluble. I will have to clean this up right away before anything else gets stuck in this nasty goop."

Dugan knelt by the baby rabbit. Suzie got close to sniff him, but Dugan pushed her away. The poor rabbit shook until Gina was afraid it would have a heart attack. The large man looked ridiculous hovering over the tiny creature, but Gina couldn't help her own heart pitter-pattering as she closely observed how gently and reverently he treated the small mammal. *I get to see the beast master at work in his element.*

Dugan crooned to the small rabbit. "It's all right, little guy. Soon you will be as free as the sun is bright."

He took out his water bottle and dumped small amounts near the rabbit's feet. He let the water sit for a few moments, then he gently picked up the squirmy bunny and dried the excess goop off his feet with the hem of his shirt.

He looked at Suzie sternly. "Stay." Then he let the small rabbit hop off into the forest. Dugan directed Gina around the sticky slime, and they continued their walk around the perimeter. They stopped at a cave door, and Dugan went around to the side. There was a little metal panel with a riddle on it. *The eagle, the greater wax moth, the bear, the catfish, the manatee. The greatest of all are these.*

Gina was reading the riddle and puzzling it over while Dugan typed a word into a keypad to punch in letters or numbers. "Dugan, what does..." Before she could finish asking about the riddle, the door slid open, and freezing cold water poured out the door, washing them both back against the compound's wall.

Chapter 9

Stalagmite Stomp

Dugan

Shaking off the water like his dog, Dugan regained his composure first. Suzie ran over and licked him on the face to reassure herself that everything was all right. "Back up, Suzie Q. Let me get up. I'm fine." He gently pushed the dog away and moved over to Gina.

The poor girl was probably terrified of this island. Already one of Jackson's traps had injured her ankle when it dragged her across the jungle floor. He noticed her pitch had raised a few decibels as she started asking suspicious questions about all the traps and riddles they kept coming across on the island, and now a malfunction in the cave entrance to the control room had washed her out. He was just getting to know her, but it wouldn't have surprised him if she ran away from this crazy island as fast as she could. Any sane person would.

Dugan was still trying to puzzle out why she stayed in the fallen-down treehouse instead of his nice cozy cottage. He didn't mind camping out with her, but it concerned him. Was she afraid to be in a cabin alone with him? He would never take advantage of a woman, but apparently, he needed to work extra hard to win this woman over. He really liked Gina. If he could gain her trust, at least they could be friends. She was way too out of his league for them to be anything more.

Gina was sitting up, wiping water off her face. A small silver fish flapped on top of her head. Dugan reached out and plucked the fish off and threw it to the side before reaching out a hand to help her up. "Well, that could have been dangerous if someone had been stuck inside when the electricity went out. Stay out here a moment while I turn the water pump off."

Without waiting for a reply, Dugan walked into the cave to figure out what caused the malfunction. He walked over to a small pool and watched as it slowly spilled water onto the cave floor again. It didn't surprise him when the very independent woman he was with walked in only a few feet behind him. She was looking around but touched nothing. He saw her studying the wall of paintings of Indigenous people and animals. "Are those paintings original to the area?"

Dugan shook his head. "No, they're something Nathan painted when he turned the back entrance of his control room into a giant puzzle. This entrance takes a while, so I don't normally come this way unless I'm doing a routine check or I need to fix something, like the light bulb in this room."

He pointed to a stalagmite on the floor that didn't quite match the ones surrounding it. "This is a pressure switch that releases the water in that pool over there so that the water drains and someone can climb down to the bottom. Normally, there is a hole that allows overflow to escape into a natural underground stream, but it seems to have gotten blocked. Would you mind activating this switch every few minutes while I go down there to clear it out?"

Gina wrapped her arms around herself and nodded. "Sure. I'll help however I can."

He needed to work fast. That poor woman must be so cold standing there soaking wet in the cool cave.

Very gingerly, she moved her foot toward the fake stalagmite and jerked it away when it jiggled slightly under her foot. Dugan nodded to her encouragingly. "Go ahead and really stomp on it. It's designed to hold up to tough use."

Gina gave a grin as she stomped on it, and Dugan hurried down into the hole. This was his least favorite trap on the entire island. It seemed like a waste of time to climb down into this pool and collect a stone saber-tooth tiger at the bottom, and it always got his feet wet. Besides, the steps dug into the side of the pool were designed with a much smaller person in mind.

Water drained away from the pool as Dugan climbed down about a quarter of the way of the hole to study the overflow area. There was nothing obvious blocking it. Before he could examine it further, he heard a loud click of the front door locking back into place. He climbed back out of the hole, but it was hard going in his wide boots, and he slipped several times, slowing him down. "Gina? Is everything all right?"

Wide-eyed, Gina looked around over at him. "I'm sorry. While you were down there, I was looking around. I touched the door, and it automatically shut."

Dugan gave an enormous sigh. "That's all right. I never told you not to touch it. Nathan has it rigged to shut and lock from several trigger points in different areas of this room for anyone who doesn't know what they're doing in here. Again, another place to keep trespassers immobilized until I can escort unwanted guests off the island. We will just have to leave the long way through the control room we were in before. Don't worry. Even with this blockage, we are in no danger. You just need to stomp on the pressure switch again to drain the water, and I can retrieve the saber-tooth tiger statue from the bottom of the pool. It's the key to leaving this room."

Calming, Gina nodded. "I'm sure glad I have you with me on this one. Although, this seems like a lot of work to get through a door. How does Nathan come up with these traps, anyway?"

Shrugging, Dugan said, "I don't know where he gets inspiration for all of his traps and riddles, but I have seen him researching Egyptian pyramids and tombs. I honestly think he often just likes the excuse to tinker. Are you ready to give this another try so we can get out of here and warm you up?"

Gina stomped on the fake stalagmite, but nothing happened. "Dugan, it didn't work. Do I have the right one?"

Dugan's face turned white as he watched the water collect at their feet. "Yeah, that's the right one. Let me try it." He activated the pressure switch, but nothing happened.

Now they were in trouble.

Chapter 10

Saber-tooth to the Rescue

Gina

Dugan held both of Gina's arms and looked deeply into her eyes. "Gina, I don't want to scare you, but I need you to listen to me carefully. Now the release isn't working, and I wasn't able to fix the clog, so we have to work quickly. This room is filling up slowly, so we have some time before we run out of oxygen, but it will just keep getting harder to get that saber-tooth."

Gina's wide eyes looked back at him, but instead of getting upset and simpering as he expected, she squared her jaw and nodded to him. She looked ready to take on the world. "I'm ready. What do you need me to do?"

Dugan pointed to the pool. "I'm going to dive into that pool and bring up the saber-tooth tiger and hand it to you. It will take me a few minutes to get out, so I'm just going to hand you the statue to place on that shelf up above the rock wall painting. There are four notches that the statue's feet fit into. It *should* unlock that back door. Sound good?"

Frowning, Gina looked at him and then over at the pool. "Why don't I get the saber-tooth? I'm a pretty good swimmer, and I have a feeling I will maneuver a lot better than you down there."

Throwing up his arms, Dugan said, "It's dangerous. Listen, there's no time to argue. Just be ready."

"I won't argue, and I'm ready." Gina ran over and dove into the pool. The water muffled the sound of Dugan calling her name, filling her ears. She used all her strength to move her arms and kick her feet to get to the bottom. At one point, she accidentally banged her injured foot against the wall, making it smart, but that just meant Dugan would have hardly been able to move at all down there.

She was running out of oxygen, but she was so close that she knew a little more perseverance would get her there. She reached out and touched the statue, wrapping her hand around its waist. It didn't budge. She wasn't expecting it to be so heavy. Lungs burning for air, Gina swam back toward the surface.

At the top of the pool, Gina gasped for air as she enjoyed letting it fill her lungs again. She saw Dugan pacing back and forth, sloshing through a few inches of water that was collecting on the cave floor.

"Gina, you shouldn't have gone in there. You could have drowned! You weren't able to get it? Come on out and I'll try."

Gina practiced taking a few deep breaths. "No, I've got this. I'm having a hard time maneuvering down there. I don't know how you could even turn around and swim back toward the surface after you got the statue." She gave him a broad smile. Gina wished their lives weren't in danger, but a part of her was loving this adventure after being so cooped up in Maxwell's house.

Gina took a deep breath and dove again. She was running out of air when she neared the bottom again, but this time, she had her body prepared to somersault near the bottom of the pool. In one motion, she was able to scoop up the statue while pushing her feet off the ground and zooming upwards.

Unfortunately, the heavy statue wouldn't let her go very far. Gina began releasing bits of her air to avoid gasping in a breath of water. She used the stairs built into the side of the pool to continue pushing herself upwards. She could see a light not far in front of her, but she just couldn't make it.

Unable to help herself, she took a gulp of water. To her surprise, muscular arms grasped her shoulders and pulled her the last bit of the way out of the hole. Dugan cradled her above the water as she coughed and gasped for air, dropping the statue onto the floor in the foot-deep water beneath them.

Finally catching her breath, Gina continued to heave as Dugan gently patted her back. She looked up to see Dugan's furrowed brows that had fresh water dripping off them from him leaning down into the depths of the pool to save her. He held her tightly against his broad chest. "Are you all right? That was a close one. I almost didn't think you were going to make it."

Oddly, she felt more secure in Dugan's arms in the middle of a slowly flooding room than she ever did in Maxwell's. "Did I get it? Please tell me I didn't drop it back into the pool." Gina sat up and looked around frantically.

Dugan pulled it up out of the water that was now about a foot and a half high. "It's right here. You did it. You saved us. Now, let's use it to get out of here." Dugan carried the statue over to a small overhang and placed the feet in the notches. Immediately, a door beside the rock paintings slid open and the water at their feet seeped away.

Dugan motioned for her to follow him. "Come on. Let's get you taken care of, and I'll come back with the proper supplies to fix this room later. Be careful of your step. All the water from that room is making the rocks out here extra slippery."

Gina stepped out into a cave tunnel, and the motion immediately activated dim lights along the corridor. Unable to stop shivering and with a hurt foot, she did her best to keep up with Dugan as he made his way down deeper into the ground.

Eventually, they came to a ladder that led up to a trapdoor of sorts. "Go up. That's the control room up there. I'll go behind you in case you fall."

Gina was about to argue that she was perfectly fine going up by herself, but after seeing the concerned look on Dugan's face, all arguments left her. The day had already had enough excitement. She climbed up and pushed the door out of the way until she entered the small kitchenette, where Dugan had found them drinks and snacks to munch on while they visited the control room earlier.

Dugan retrieved a blanket and wrapped it around her. "So, how are you feeling? We already had a lot of adventure for today, so we can head back to my cottage or your treehouse to rest, or we can get you settled in Nathan's compound. I can finish everything else later."

Gina smiled. "It's not even noon. I think we should continue to the compound. I have to admit, I'm pretty excited to see the kitchen I'll be working in."

Dugan led her from the control room to the rear entrance of Nathan's compound. There, Suzie met them, tail wagging vigorously.

At the back of the compound, there was a large metal door, and Dugan opened a digital console next to it. He smiled to himself when it lit up. "Like a bird building a nest, at least I knew how to get this working again." He put his eye close to an iris scanner of some type, where he blinked rapidly.

Curious, Gina asked, "What are you doing? Won't that make it hard for the scanner to read your eyes?"

Dugan smiled as the door clicked. He turned a knob and entered, Gina close behind him. "Part of the security I installed in this entryway is a combination of an eye scan and a blinking code to enter. Blinking the incorrect code sets off all kinds of alarms. If you remember, I mentioned the front entrance is double-gated so it can trap someone trying to get in. Just stay in the compound until I get you set up, and then you can come and go as you please."

Gina stopped and looked back at the door she just passed through. Her heart raced.

I'm trapped. This is the catch. What if Dugan's not really such a nice guy and never lets me go? What if that was all just an act? He trapped me here, just like Maxwell trapped me in his house. Is there no escape? Is Riley's Paradise Island just the next trap I've walked into?

Chapter 11

My Favorite Weapon: The Soup Spoon

G ina

Gina took a few deep breaths, calming herself. *Dugan is trustworthy. He has given me no reason to doubt him. I'm sure he will get me set up to come and go as I please as soon as he is able, just like he promised.*

Dugan led Gina through a few hallways, their wet shoes making squelching noises whenever they walked on the tile. Gina was chafing, but at least her ankle was feeling better. As usual, she kept her minor discomforts to herself. Eventually, they came to a large laundry room.

"Here's a washer and dryer. I have to go clean up that slime we found outside and then I'll be back to show you around." Dugan quickly turned and left, with Suzie right at his heels.

Oh, man. She forgot to get a change of clothing from Dugan before he left. The clothes she was in were so wet, cold, and uncomfortable. She was dying to take them off, but she couldn't bring herself to just walk around naked. *That would give my beast master the wrong impression about me. He's an intriguing man. He's quiet and compassionate. Not like any man I have ever known before. He may not be handsome in a traditional sense, but he has a manly, woodsy aura to him.*

Gina shook her head to clear her musing. *It doesn't matter if the man looks like a monkey or an Adonis. I'm never dating again, so it shouldn't matter.* She looked around for an idea of what she should wear. She saw a sundress hanging on a drying rack.

This must belong to the mistress of the house, Brianna. I know it's rather presumptuous of me to borrow it. If I wash it and return it, she will never know, right? Gina slipped off all of her wet clothes and threw them into the washing machine, including her undergarments. She slid on the sundress. It was slightly too big, but it covered all the important parts.

She turned on the washer and looked around for Dugan. He wasn't back yet.

Gina walked out of the laundry room and took a left turn. She passed a living room and an office. The decor was sparse, inconsistent, and very masculine. If she didn't know that Nathan had a wife, she would have thought this was a bachelor pad. She wondered why Brianna hadn't put a more feminine touch on things, but Dugan did mention that they were only recently married. Maybe she hadn't had a chance yet.

Gina's thoughts went back to the day of her interview. Nathan had asked her to meet him in a little seashore restaurant. He explained he was looking for someone to cook full-time for himself, his wife, and his young daughter on Riley's Paradise Island. It had seemed like a blessing, the perfect way to disappear from Maxwell's constant overbearing presence.

To her surprise, he'd asked her if she would mind cooking them lunch as part of the interview. He said he'd noticed she didn't have a lot of experience on her resume other than a waitressing job in high school, but her enthusiasm had impressed him during their phone conversation, so he wanted to give her a chance. Of course, on the island, she would have whatever supplies she needed, but for the sake of time, he was hoping she could whip up something in twenty minutes. Everything was arranged with the restaurant owner to rent out the kitchen if she was interested. He called it a hands-on interview.

Gina's thoughts came back to the present as she walked into the next room. She saw the kitchen, or at least what used to be a kitchen. A tree must have fallen from the storm, breaking the window. The storm had filled the room with branches, leaves, and dirt. She even thought she spotted a bird's nest sitting on the kitchen table.

The countertops and stove seemed unharmed, other than being filthy. Gina opened the refrigerator. It was mostly empty but had a slightly sour odor, presumably from when the power was off.

She stepped over to the window. There was a lot of water damage where rain had poured straight in. Water damage had caused the window seal to warp, and the whole thing would need to be replaced. The tile floor held enough water to form a small pond, but it looked like it would survive after a bit of cleaning.

A door opening up to the pantry was ajar, and Gina went to take a peek. Immediately, she backed up as half a dozen monkeys started jumping up and down and howling at her excitedly. One even threw some of the dry noodles it was eating out of a box.

Gina grabbed a nearby broom and shooed the angry creatures back out the window. Then she set about cleaning up the countertop and stove with disinfectant she found under the sink. She went back into the pantry and almost jumped out of her skin as a mouse ran right over her foot. *Where is the beast master now? I think the only food safe in here is in metal cans.*

She grabbed a few cans of soup and went back to the kitchen, washing a pot, and starting up a simple meal. She whistled as she worked. She had always felt the most content in kitchens. Even in the middle of the storms of her life, it had always centered her.

She was feeling so relaxed, like everything was finally right in the world. That was when the growling started. A hair-raising, fierce growl came from behind her. She spun around with only her soup spoon to protect herself.

Chapter 12

The BeastMaster

Dugan

Dugan walked toward the kitchen area, his hungry stomach following his nose to something that smelled delicious. He stopped short in the doorway. Subconsciously, he noted the room looked like a disaster. He knew that was where the focus of his attention should be, but despite the surrounding chaos, he couldn't take his eyes off Gina.

She stood by the stove in a sundress that hung loosely over her thin frame. Without the figure to fill it out, the front was low and barely covered her breasts. The way the thin fabric clung to her shapely bottom showed him she wasn't wearing anything underneath.

Dugan's brain was having trouble firing on all cylinders until he heard a low growl coming from near the broken window. He stepped into the room to assess the danger, but before he could do anything, he saw Gina spin around and square off against a raccoon with only a soup spoon to protect herself.

Who is this fiercely independent and captivating woman? I was perfectly happy being by myself before she came. Now I don't know if I can ever go back to the way things were.

Dugan snapped into action. He grabbed a nearby broom and whistled for Suzie, who he'd left sniffing something down the hall. The dog came running, and as soon as she entered the kitchen, the raccoon took off out the window. Suzie sniffed around and rooted out a monkey as well.

When everything settled down, Dugan said, "Like the first pear from a fruit tree, that food smells amazing."

Gina gave him her angelic smile, and his heart melted into goo. He would have done anything to protect this woman.

"Thanks," Gina said. "I only had some canned goods to work with, but I was hoping the extra spices I added would upgrade it a bit. Just wait until I get fresh supplies."

Dugan felt the urge to ignore all other responsibilities and get her all the fresh ingredients she desired. He wanted to do anything to make her happy. *I'll be a bear after his first taste of honey. Am I hopeless? Am I destined to pine after a woman I can't have?*

He thought of the harsh rejections he'd received as a younger man the few times he was brave enough to ask a girl out. A curled lip of disgust was enough to dissuade any man, and that was before he was emotionally scarred from his days in the military. There was just no way a woman that beautiful would be interested in an antisocial brute like himself. *I just have to stay away. Maybe it will be easier once the other employees come and it's not just the two of us.*

Dugan changed the subject, trying to distract his thoughts. "After we have something to eat, why don't I get you set up with the compound's security, so you have free rein in this place?"

Gina clutched her hands together as she softly said, "Thank you." It was an oddly appreciative response to something simple that he had already promised her he would do.

After taking a big whiff of the stew, his belly grumbled. "Unfortunately, after I get you situated, I must be off. I have to release Pongo and Chee Chee from destroying my cottage and start working on cleaning out the main paths while I have daylight. We have a lot more to do on this island than we have time to do it. If I can get the construction crew here that I have waiting on standby, at least we will have help."

Dugan looked at the wrecked window, a large puddle, and debris covering the entire room. Finally, taking it all in, he got out his cell phone and snapped a picture to send as an update to Nathan.

"You know, you really don't have to sleep out in the treehouse unless you want to. There are some spare bedrooms upstairs that you can borrow for the time being. You can even use my room here at the compound. With the pup and monkey at my cottage, I can't leave them unattended for long."

Gina wouldn't look him in the eye as she responded firmly. "No. I enjoy having my space."

Dugan shrugged. "All right, then I will leave you to your cooking skills as I take inventory of the rest of the house. I'll be upstairs. Give me a holler if you need anything."

Dugan had to physically pull himself away from the woman that was captivating all his thoughts. *I need to focus on the job at hand.* He made a mental tally of the impossible tasks he had to accomplish. Messing up was not an option. He had to prove himself to Nathan.

Let's see. I have a few days to get the island safe enough to invite the construction crew. They need time to fix up the house and build an entire employee housing complex. Which would be a hard task even if we weren't short on time and working on an island far from supplies. Then I have to invite all the employees to the island and have them trained and running smoothly by the time Nathan steps foot on the island.

All of that, and he wasn't even able to schedule in time for things to go wrong or the fact that, honestly, he wasn't the best at managing people. He was more of a lone wolf and was much better with animals. A bunch of workers milling about made him feel like soon there would be too many roosters in the henhouse.

If I hadn't screwed up a bunch of months ago and caught that smuggler right away before he took Brianna, maybe I could have kept this island mostly to myself... except maybe they could have still invited Gina. As it was, Nathan insisted he needed help to run the island smoothly, and while Dugan agreed, he wasn't particularly pleased about it. He would have rather trained a hundred dogs to help him watch over the island than have two people added to his security team, even if they were more than qualified.

Grumpily, he walked up the stairs. Most of the bedrooms were fine, except for one of the spares; the one Brianna was using as her bedroom until her wedding night. This was where the tree fell and crunched in the roof. A few of her glass figurines lay broken on the floor.

Dugan snapped a few more pictures with his cellphone. He salvaged a few more figurines and what looked like some of Brianna's glass-blowing supplies. *I hope she's not too upset about the broken baubles. At least I know Nathan is a good man and will replace any damaged supplies.*

He moved the last of her things to another room to keep them safe and dry until he could get this room fixed. He was just about to head back to the kitchen when he heard Gina screaming. Both he and Suzie bolted down the stairs. He hoped they would be in time.

Chapter 13

Snake-Flavored Tarts

G ina

A loud cry escaped Gina's lips as she jumped back in surprise. Coiled beside the canned cherries she'd been reaching for in the pantry, a green snake sat silently and perfectly still. The place was feeling more like a zoo than a kitchen.

Staring at the snake, Gina tried to figure out how she would get it out of her pantry, and she wished she could identify if this tropical snake was venomous or not. She could find Dugan to take care of it, but what if it wandered off as soon as she left it out of sight? She didn't want to be constantly scared that it would pop out at her. It was only a week since the storm let up. How many creatures had moved in during that time?

After she got rid of this little fellow, she would definitely need to do a thorough sweep of the room to make sure she didn't miss any other "friends" and insist that they put up a board to cover the broken window immediately. She couldn't work while being constantly interrupted by the local wildlife.

A moment later, Dugan came charging into the pantry so fast that he almost knocked her over. Suzie was hot on his heels. His enormous form made the generously sized pantry feel tiny. Breathing heavily, he took a deep breath when he saw her. "Gina! Are you all right? I heard you scream and came right away."

Ducking her head and sucking on her teeth, Gina pointed to the snake. "Sorry. That little guy really surprised me. I didn't mean to worry you. Do you know if it's venomous?"

Glancing over at the snake, he shook his head. "No, he's harmless, but give him some space because he still bites." He looked back at Gina and gave her a half-smile. "After I saw you fearlessly take on a raccoon with a soup spoon, I figured the only thing that would have made you scream was a bear. Here, keep an eye on him while I get something to catch him."

Dugan left the room, and the room felt bare. For a bit of a backwards hermit, she really liked him. It was good that she was making a friend, but she needed to be very clear that they could never be more. She wasn't willing to risk her heart again after being burned so badly last time.

A few moments later, Dugan came back with a trashcan and a pasta spoon. Slowly, the beast master nudged and lifted the snake until it was in the can. Then he handed her the spoon. There was no way she was going to cook with that again, even after being cleaned. "I'm going to drop this fellow off outside and bring in a piece of wood to block off that broken window. How soon will that delicious-smelling meal be ready? Like a hound after a hare, it's making my mouth water."

Gina chuckled. His sayings were growing on her. "Actually, the stew is ready. I was just in here because I thought I would whip up some cherry tarts for dessert."

Dugan lifted an eyebrow and licked his lips. "Gina, you are a gem. I'll be back in five minutes." For a large man, he could move awfully fast when properly motivated.

Taking a box of just-add-water baking mix and the can of cherry filling to the kitchen, Gina again wished she had access to fresh ingredients. She wanted to do something nice for Dugan, who had only shown her patience and kindness since she arrived, but the results could only be so good with such limited supplies. She would just have to surprise him with a fancy meal after their first supply run arrived.

As promised, five minutes later, Dugan was hammering a large piece of plywood over the broken window. She popped the tarts she'd made into the oven, set a timer, and spooned out two gigantic bowls of stew.

She was delivering the bowls to the kitchen table when Dugan walked over and sat down heavily. He took one bowl from Gina and took a large whiff of his bowl before setting it down in front of him. "What did you put in here? This doesn't smell like the canned stew I normally eat."

Smiling, Gina sat down across from him. "I had little to work with, but there was a nice collection of dried herbs in the cupboards that I added. I hope you like it."

Dugan took a large spoonful. "Well, I'll be a babe at my first meal. This is delicious. If I didn't know you were out of fresh supplies, I would think it was homemade." A touch of pink colored Gina's cheeks as she watched him dig into his meal with enthusiasm. Without another word, he finished up his bowl. "Do you mind if I grab some more?"

After they finished up their meal and enjoyed their dessert, Dugan led her out to the main portcullis gate. He opened a small control panel and typed away at it for a few minutes while Gina watched, unable to follow what he was doing. Eventually, he stared into a retinal scanner and blinked ridiculously before turning toward her.

"All right, I have it all set up for your first code to help you come and go from Nathan's compound as you please. I'm going to make your first one easy to help you get used to the system, but when I change it in a few months, it will be a lot more complex. What you are going to do is type into this number pad one, two, three, and then put your eyes up to the scanner. Blink once, pause for a second, blink twice, pause for a second, and blink three times. If you don't start your blinking pattern, it will activate a code-red procedure that will temporarily open the gate but then shut it soon after, creating a trap."

Gina followed his instructions until she felt comfortable leaving and entering the facility at will. Dugan gave her a big smile. "You look like you're good to go. I have to head over to my cottage and let out Pongo and Chee Chee, and then I'm off to keep working on cleaning up these trails. Do you need anything? You can spend the night here and I'll see you tomorrow."

Kneeling down to pet Suzie, Gina looked up at Dugan with wide eyes. Her previous experiences with her ex-boyfriend had left her doubtful that Dugan would agree to her helping him, but she figured she should at least give him a chance to let her come with him before she snuck out on her own. All the gates around the compound were making her feel claustrophobic, and she needed a break from this place. "Why don't I come and help you clear out the trails? I plan to sleep in the fallen treehouse, and I would like to explore a bit more of the island. Besides, it won't take me too long to clean up the kitchen tomorrow."

Dugan pursed his lips and was silent for a while. "I don't like the idea of you getting hurt out here, but I can't exactly keep you cooped up here, either. If you want to get out and explore the island, I guess I'd prefer you do it with me than by yourself. These traps are dangerous and misfiring after the storm, so please be careful."

Gina smiled at how easily Dugan agreed. She had expected him to argue and demand she stay back. It looked like she wouldn't need to sneak out by herself after all.

"Lead the way."

She was curious to see what the cottage of this beast master would look like. *There is so much I still don't know about Dugan, and there is a lot you can learn by how someone keeps their personal space.*

Chapter 14

Bachelor Pad

Dugan

Unsure of himself for the first time in a very long time, Dugan kept glancing back at Gina. He didn't know why it was so important to him, but he really hoped she liked his cottage. It was small and simple, the complete opposite of Nathan's mansion, but to him, it was the perfect home.

He heard waves crashing against the shore before the clearing around his cottage came into view. There were large pits in a V-shape all around the jungle entrance to his home. Usually, they were indistinguishable from the ground around them and fell when trod upon to trap interlopers, but like everything else on the island, it wasn't working quite right.

Suzie zoomed up to the cottage and entered a doggie door that led inside. He could hear Pongo barking excitedly from the fenced-in training yard that Dugan had left him in that morning while he did more sensitive work. The pup still needed more training before he had free rein of the island.

Gina frowned at the holes, and a part of him wanted to fix the traps immediately, or even start filling them up with dirt to see her smile again. "What are these holes for?"

He shrugged. "When I told Nathan that I needed a bit of space out here, he insisted on adding some traps around my cottage so trespassers couldn't sneak up on me in my sleep. I'll fix this and you won't even be able to tell where the fake ground differs from the real ground, but with so much to do, it isn't dangerous as it is, so it's low on my priority list."

Turning around and walking backward the last few steps to his cabin, he grinned at Gina. "This is my home. You are always welcome."

He opened the door to his one-room cottage and held it wide for Gina to enter. He watched her eyes grow wide as they took in the five-hundred-square-foot room of sparse simple furniture, a kitchenette, and an enormous bed. There weren't many decorations on the walls, but the gigantic fireplace and dark wood trim gave it a cozy feel. Since his cottage sat right on the edge of the jungle, he had a wide window that overlooked the shoreline and out onto the sea on one side and another overlooking the jungle on the other. He loved it. It felt like he could be outside while still having shelter out of the elements.

He walked over to a large container on the floor and opened it up. Immediately, Chee Chee scampered out and chattered. Dugan talked back. "I'm sorry I had to put you there, but last time I tried to leave you for even a little, you and Pongo had all of my furniture knocked over and cabinets emptied. Let me get you something to eat and then we'll go on an adventure. Does that sound good?"

Remembering Gina, Dugan looked at his boots, embarrassed that this beautiful woman caught him talking to a monkey. He started to cut up some fruit for Chee Chee. "I'm going to feed these guys and then we can be off. I'm clearing out the main path going from the docks to Nathan's compound first so that I can invite the construction crew to start. Don't go wandering around too much farther on your own. It might be a bit before I get everything safe again. Nathan is a good man. While he likes to make lots of riddles and traps, everything is safe, unless they're malfunctioning like they are now."

Dugan opened the door that led to the fenced-in outside training area. Immediately, Pongo rushed in, wagging his whole body along with his tail and greeting them. Dugan was dying to know what Gina was thinking. She was being awfully quiet. Did she find his simple living boring? He poured out some dog food into two separate bowls, and Suzie and Pongo enthusiastically chowed down. "Do you want to help me fix the dock? We're going to need it to unload construction supplies."

Gina was studying the single photo he had hanging on his wall, a picture of him dressed in his full uniform with a woman who looked like his mother hugging him after basic training. "Sure. I'm ready whenever you are." She looked down at the dogs. "Or at least whenever they are."

Dugan gathered a toolbox and handed Gina a towel. "Here. I have a feeling we're going to get wet." Chee Chee clambered up on his shoulder when he'd finished eating, and the dogs wagged their tails eagerly. Dugan opened the front door of his cabin and Pongo took off like a flash, while Suzie stayed right by Dugan's side. "It looks like you were excited to get out, now, weren't you, boy? Although we still have a lot of work to do on getting you to heel."

They made their way down to Otter Cove. Gina pointed to a platform about halfway up a tree that had a small ladder leading to it. "What is that for?"

The hunting stand was one of the more normal aspects of Riley's Paradise Island, so Dugan talked while he walked. "That's just a spot where a hunter can sit, but Nathan and I strategically placed it so I can monitor the cove and surrounding jungle without being spotted myself. Honestly, it's mainly used by Nathan and his daughter for bird-watching. It's a fantastic view up there."

They kept walking until they came to the broken docks. Dugan stopped and put his finger up to his mouth. He gave a soft whistle for the dogs, and they ran over and sat silently at his feet. He pointed toward the shore, where he spotted two otters. They were playfully sliding down the mud of the bank into the water and wrestling about. Dugan smiled to see how enraptured Gina looked watching the scene. He found he couldn't take his eyes off her, just as she didn't look away from the playful critters.

Eventually, Pongo could stand it no longer and barked. The two otters disappeared, leaving no sign of themselves but a ripple in the water. Pongo ran up to splash in the water as he and Gina walked the rest of the way to the shore. He surveyed the damage to see if he could fix it without getting additional wood from near his cottage. A chunk of the dock remained in place, with a few loose boards scattered about. "Do you mind walking around on the shore to see if you can find the few boards that aren't lying around? I'll get started on putting this thing back together. A few well-placed nails should have it temporarily serviceable again."

Gina gave him an enormous smile, seemingly delighted by the idea. "Sure thing. I'll see what I can find."

He watched her walk away, periodically picking up a rock or a shell and throwing it into the water. In a way, he wished that no one else would join them on the island. The Rileys were rich. Couldn't they just buy another island? He could live his whole life here joyfully and peacefully if he had Gina with him. Tearing his eyes away, he waded into the water to drag out a chunk that had come loose from shore and got to work reassembling it.

He was making good progress when Gina came back. She had a huge grin on her face and was holding two planks that looked like they belonged to the dock. She laid down the wood and held out her hands. "You will never believe what I found on the shore!"

Chapter 15

The Cowboy

G ina

Gina was having a hard time containing her excitement as she held out a small box to Dugan. The box was about one inch wide and two inches long, and its creator had decorated it with geometric symbols, but there was no apparent way to open it.

Dugan picked up the box and gently wiped the remaining sand off it. "Huh, I'm not sure how that got down here to the beach, but I'll tell you what. If you can figure out what it does without breaking it, I'll show you what it goes to."

Gina took the box back, examining every inch in the sunlight. "What is it? Why are you being so cryptic?"

Shrugging, Dugan gave her a half-smile. "Like a lyrebird mimics its neighbors, I guess Nathan is rubbing off on me. Want to try it?"

Slipping the box into her pocket, Gina couldn't help smiling back. She was having such a pleasant time that she almost wished this camaraderie of just the two of them would last forever. "Yeah, I'm up to the challenge. Although, wouldn't it surprise you if I figure out what it goes to first?"

Dugan chuckled and went back to work. They finished fixing the dock by the evening, when Dugan escorted her back to the fallen treehouse. It began to rain, and Dugan held the towel over her head. "Do you want to come back to my cottage tonight? I would prefer you not to sleep out in the rain, and I promise you can have the bed while I sleep on the floor."

Gina shook her head. "I wouldn't dream of making you sleep on the floor." Realizing that he might misconstrue her comment, she amended it. "I mean, go back to your cottage, and I'm happy to stay in this treehouse. It looked sturdy enough to keep out the rain, and I'll use the cot you brought me. It's safely stowed inside away from the rain. I'll be fine until morning."

Dugan frowned but didn't argue. When they arrived at the cottage, he climbed inside and checked to make sure the place was dry, but then he just stood there, staring at her. He held a towel over her head while rain dripped from his own sopping-wet hair. "Like a rabbit to its den, I guess I should go now."

He didn't move.

Gina smiled. "Thank you for a great day. I promise I'll tackle cleaning up the kitchen tomorrow, and I'll make you something else tasty to eat too."

He leaned closer, and Gina felt a thrill rush through her. *Is he going to kiss me?* She fought her desire, knowing that it would only lead to complications she wasn't ready to deal with. She was still reeling from escaping the last guy.

Before he got too close, he stopped and whispered, "Good night, Gina." Then he awkwardly tried to open the window of the treehouse with his elbow while still holding the towel. Gina laughed and helped him open it before climbing inside. Before securing the window, she whispered back in the same sensual tone, "Good night, Dugan."

***

Knock, knock, knock.

"Excuse me, ma'am. Were you stranded here in the storm? Are you all right? Can I take you back to the mainland?"

Gina opened her eyes to spy a very handsome, concerned man looking at her through the window of the fallen treehouse she used as a door. He was slim, with short blond hair and a bit of stubble around his jawline. He wore a flannel shirt with the top few buttons undone and topped it off with a cowboy hat. *Does that man think he's a cowboy? If so, he's far from home.*

Gina sat up in the cot she had moved into her temporary home. "No, I work here. I'm the cook. Who are you?"

The man grumbled. "This better not be the nice employee housing Nathan was telling me about when he convinced me to move here full-time. My name's Thomas. I'm in charge of Nathan's secret garden, and I care for all the animals up there. Right now, I'm here to see how the garden fared the storm, so I can start bringing the animals back."

He took his hat off and used it to fan himself. He raised an eyebrow and gave her a slow half-smile that could stop a woman's heartbeat. "Believe me, it was no simple task to evacuate all those critters by boat."

Thomas stepped out of the way as Gina moved to exit through the window. She spotted Pongo bounding down the path. He happily greeted Gina and Thomas. His tail wagged excitedly as he gave them lots of kisses.

Thomas knelt down and rubbed Pongo's sides. "Hey, boy. You are getting so big. When I saw you before the storm, you were half that size!" Pongo soaked up the attention and then barked wildly, looking back down the path for Dugan.

Eventually, an exhausted-looking Dugan came down the path. Trusty Suzie was walking by his side, and Chee Chee looked like he was asleep, sitting on his shoulder. Thomas greeted him cheerily. "It looks like you stayed and weathered the storm! You look horrible."

Dugan rubbed at his eyes. "I didn't stay here during the storm, but there's just so much to do that when it stopped raining last night, I worked through the night. I thought maybe I could get the construction crew out here tomorrow, but I'm regretting that decision right now." He looked back and forth between Thomas and Gina and raised an eyebrow. "I see you met Nathan's new cook, Gina."

Thomas glanced over at Gina. "Yes, we were just getting to know each other. She was showing off the palatial employee housing options."

Dugan tried to smile but must have been too tired because it ended up looking more like a grimace. "I'm surprised you're back already. I don't have everything safe yet, you know."

"I was going to find out the status of the secret garden. Did you have time to look at it?"

Dugan shook his head.

Thomas looked at Dugan pityingly. "I'll tell you what, why don't you call the construction crew and get them lined up to come out tomorrow? Then take a few hours' nap. You will not be good to anyone in your current state. I'll take a look at the secret garden and then come back and help you clear the main walkways."

Dugan said, "I feel like a fish in the desert. Thank you. I would appreciate the help."

Thomas looked over at Gina. "Would you like to come see the secret garden with me? If you haven't seen it yet, you're in for a real treat."

Gina saw Dugan stiffen out of the corner of her eye, but he remained silent. *Is there some sort of contention between my beast master and the cowboy? They seemed like friends ready to work together on a project just moments ago. It's just an innocent walk.*

Gina smiled at Thomas. "Yes, I would like to get to know the island a bit more. I need to clean the kitchen, but I really can't do a thorough clean of the house until after the construction crew comes through. Will we be back in time so I can clean up and whip something together for lunch for all of us?"

Thomas grinned from ear to ear. "Since I know you're making lunch, I wouldn't want to miss it!"

Dugan watched their exchange and then shambled off into the forest. He called Pongo to him, who came rushing out of the woods.

Thomas stopped him. "We can take the pup with us if you want. His energy never stops. That way, you can take a nap without him waking you up ten times."

Dugan slowly nodded. Thomas whistled for Pongo to come to him, and Pongo stopped between the two men. He looked back and forth, confused, not sure who to go with. Finally, Dugan pointed to Thomas. "Go with Thomas, Pongo. I will see you soon."

Gina watched the exhausted Dugan turn and walk away. She had never seen him look so defeated before. She had an unsettling desire to chase after him and comfort him. He looked like it would feel so safe and comforting to cuddle up next to him.

She needed to get her head back on straight. Even if she was looking for romance, which she was not, trying to get close to that man would be like trying to cuddle a porcupine. Oh, no. There she was, thinking like her beast master again.

She would keep her distance. Thomas seemed a lot safer. While he was handsome, she didn't feel the same magnetic draw she felt to the man currently walking away from her.

Chapter 16

Secret Garden

Gina

Following Thomas, Gina couldn't help staring at the surrounding wildlife. A large rodent crashed through the brush to her right and Pongo chased it, while birds called out to one another above her. This truly was the most beautiful place in the world. She couldn't believe she had escaped to such a haven.

They walked through a pass between two hills that led into a valley with an enormous wall and a moat around it. The grass growing around the moat was a bit overgrown, but the lack of weeds made Gina think Thomas usually kept it very well maintained. Thomas led her around the wall and straight to a main door.

A large branch had fallen across a small bridge that crossed the moat. Thomas quickly pulled the branch away and threw it into the nearby jungle. She could now see that the bridge was comprised of four boards that led to a large stone door. Thomas pointed at them. "Be careful. You can only step on the outer two boards, or they flip and cause you to fall into the moat."

Confidently, Thomas strode across the boards, but the far right board twisted under his foot. With a yelp, it catapulted Thomas through the air and straight into the water, his cowboy hat floating gently beside him. Sitting in waist-high water, he frowned. One arm was underwater where he tried to catch himself during his fall, but the other was free to nab his hat. He positioned it back on his head, not seeming to care that water dripped from it. Pongo ran over and licked at his face until he used his free hand to push the dog away.

"Are you all right?" Gina cried as she ran to the moat. A few frogs hopped out of her path as she rushed through the high grass.

Thomas struggled to move for a few moments, but nothing under the water budged. He looked up at Gina and pursed his lips. "I'm fine, just stuck in the moat trap. Nathan installed these fasteners under here that hold things in place until someone places a certain amount of force upon them. I guess I should have checked that the branch didn't knock the bridge loose before I tried to cross it."

Full of concern, Gina knelt on the bank, trying to see into the murky water. "How can I help you get out of there?"

Thomas looked her over and scratched his head. "Honestly, there is a complicated puzzle and a few traps to be careful of that I would have to walk you through to deactivate the one I'm trapped in. I hate to ask this of you, but do you think you could navigate your way back to Dugan's cottage? I don't know how long you've been here, so if you don't know where it is, then we will just work our way through these puzzles one at a time to get you into the secret garden and deactivate this trap. Otherwise, I'm going to be here a while."

Gina tried to picture the mental map she'd created. She thought she could get from here to Nathan's compound, and yesterday she went from Nathan's compound to Dugan's cottage. "Yes, I think I should be able to get him. I'll be back soon."

She turned to Pongo and sternly told him, "Stay." The pup whined but didn't move as she got up and jogged back to the hillside pass. She heard Thomas yell behind her, "Be careful of traps!"

Back in the jungle's shade, Gina jogged until she got a stitch in her side and her mouth was getting sticky from dryness. She needed to invest in a water bottle to take around with her on these island adventures. Speed-walking now, she shook her hand triumphantly at Nathan's compound as she walked past.

Now it was time for the slightly trickier part, to get from Nathan's compound to Dugan's cottage. She rushed past the jungle, not taking in its beauty anymore. Poor Thomas was sitting there in the water, getting prunier by the minute. While she had only been gone about ten minutes thus far, did he really think it was faster to get Dugan than walk her through the puzzles? Were they that hard, or did he not believe that she could handle them?

She noticed her treehouse in the distance and groaned. She'd missed the turnoff and gone too far. Turning back, she hoped she didn't lose herself in the jungle when someone needed her to get help. She picked a turnoff that looked familiar and hoped it would lead her the right way. Feeling more confident, she picked up her pace until a snare caught her foot and she fell flat on her face. *What is wrong with this crazy island? How can the Rileys expect anyone to work here when you can't make it from one part of the island to another without being caught in a trap of some sort?*

She loosened the snare and removed her sore foot, but instead of resetting it, she wrapped it around the pole that secured it. She hobbled on until Dugan's cottage came into view. Suzie charged out from under the front porch, but after a short greeting, retreated to her shelter.

She hated to disturb the exhausted man, but she couldn't let Thomas just sit in the water for hours while Dugan slept. She limped through the maze of pits near his cottage and up the stairs. No one answered when she knocked. Did he fall asleep at Nathan's compound or somewhere else?

Before taking off to search for Dugan when he could be anywhere, she decided to double-check he wasn't in his cottage. She found a log in the nearby brush and rolled it over to the immense window that overlooked the beach. She climbed on top of it and held her hands over her eyes to cut the glare as she peered into his window. As she leaned forward, the log rolled backward, causing her to crash through the window and straight into Dugan's house.

Chapter 17

Broken Glass

The glass broke all around her as she put her hands out in front of herself to break the fall. Sharp pangs shot through her hands as the glass cut through them, and she felt something pierce her side as her legs hung uselessly outside of the window. Suzie barked wildly below them.

Quick as a flash, Dugan was there. Wearing only a pair of boxers, he scooped her up and carried her over to his bed. While slight dark circles still rimmed the bottom of his eyelids, he seemed completely alert. "Gina, are you all right? I said you were always welcome, but you know I have a door, right?"

Looking up at Dugan hovering over her, with muscles rippling beneath a hint of chest hair, Gina gulped. He felt even more enormous than normal, and everything around her smelled of his manly musk. "I think I'm okay. I'm so sorry about your window. When I earn enough money, I'll pay to have it replaced."

He examined her hands and shook his head. He breathed a little easier, and Gina saw her wounds were all fairly shallow. "Don't worry about the window. I'm just glad you're okay. What were you doing?"

Gina tried to sit up but gasped in pain and lay back down. "Can you check my side above my right hip? I think I got cut there too. Thomas is stuck in the secret garden, and I was trying to get him help. I tried knocking, but you must have slept through it because I was just checking in the window to see if you were here before I started searching all over the island for you."

Gently, Dugan lifted the hem of her shirt. Chee Chee climbed out from where he was hiding behind the bed and came over to investigate until Dugan used his hand to shoo the little monkey away. She tried to lift her head to see what he was looking at when he looked up at her face and deep into her eyes. He wiped a stray hair out of the way and whispered. "Please don't move. There is a piece of glass stuck in this wound. It's not deep, but I don't want to make it worse. Do you hurt anywhere else?"

Staying perfectly still, Gina said, "No. Just my hands and my side."

Dugan walked over to a shelf and pulled down a small container. He started pulling out bandages, antiseptic, and a small needle and suture kit. "Is Thomas in any immediate danger?"

Gina shook her head but stopped mid-movement. It was hard to lie perfectly still. "He is probably as wrinkly as a prune by now, but otherwise, he was just sitting in the water uncomfortably when I left. I told Pongo to stay with him."

Carrying his equipment over to the bed, he laid everything out beside her. "Good, then he can wait a little longer." He looked her in the eyes. "This wound isn't deep, but someone should really stitch it up immediately after we pull the glass out to make sure it doesn't keep bleeding. I have some basic field experience in treating wounds from my Army days, but I'm not a doctor. Do you trust me?"

Gina knew Dugan didn't realize how heavily his words sat upon her chest. Trust was a hard thing to earn, especially after she'd given it away too easily before. She took a moment before answering, and Dugan didn't rush her. She looked around the small room, and instead of feeling claustrophobic like she did in Maxwell's mansion, she felt safe and calm. Looking back into Dugan's eyes, she realized she had never truly trusted Maxwell to the same degree she already trusted Dugan. Deep down, she must have instinctively known all along that something was off with her ex-boyfriend.

She closed her eyes, not wanting to see what was coming next. "Yes, Dugan. I trust you with my life."

She felt Dugan's strong, calloused hand gently caress her cheek. "Don't worry, this isn't anything life-threatening. We will just have to monitor it to make sure it doesn't get infected. I have some low-dose numbing spray with my first-aid kit, but you will probably still feel this."

Gina clutched Dugan's sheets in her fists but couldn't help letting out a gasp as the glass came out and her eyes popped open. Immediately, Dugan applied pressure with some bandages. "Are you all right? I'm going to need to start the stitches next."

Twisting the sheets even tighter into her palms, Gina grimaced as a sweat broke out across her brow. "Go ahead. I'm so sorry if I'm getting blood all over your sheets."

Dugan used his free hand to pick up the sterilized needle he had prepared. "I can get new sheets. What I can't get is a new one of you."

After he stitched her up, Dugan propped a few pillows up behind her so she could sit up a bit as he grabbed her a glass of water. He even held the end of the glass while she drank. Gina had never felt so pampered and cared for before.

He sat on the bed next to her. "I only had to give you five stitches, so you can get up and walk around, but I would suggest taking it easy for a while so that you don't burst them open. While you can do some light cleaning and cooking, let me know if you need anything heavy lifted or moved and I'll help you."

He sat there staring at her, and she had to hold back the desire to place her hand upon his muscular bare chest. She looked down around herself to see what a disaster she had made of his bed. The quilt was strewn across the foot of the bed, probably from when Dugan hopped out of bed in surprise from her crash-landing. The sheets looked permanently stretched where she had grasped them and pulled with all her might into the balls of her fists. At least there wasn't a lot of blood everywhere. "I'm so sorry I destroyed your cute little cottage."

Dugan cleaned up the excess supplies that still lay around her. "When I said you were welcome anytime, I meant it. My home is your home. Just next time, if you would mind using the door, it would be a lot less clean-up after your visit. Do you mind resting here while I free Thomas?"

Sleep overcame an exhausted Gina. She couldn't keep going from the exhaustion caused by her poor sleeping arrangements over the past few nights, the pain of her wounds, running through the jungle, and all their hiking adventures over the past few days. Getting up and walking back to the secret garden was the last thing she wanted to do. She fought to keep her heavy eyelids open. "Thank you. I think I will take you up on that..."

Gina stayed aware long enough to watch as Dugan pulled on clothing but was fast asleep by the time he swept up the glass. She drifted off to sleep, barely aware as Dugan tucked her in with his quilt and laid a light kiss on her forehead before leaving.

***

Gina woke as the sun rose. She snuggled into her warm bed, not wanting to leave its comfort. She lifted her arms and stretched, when a sharp pain in her side brought all her memories of the day before back to her. Her eyes popped open, and she spotted Dugan working busily stapling a mesh screen around the opening where the window used to be.

Gina hurried out of his bed as quickly as she could without hurting herself. "Oh, Dugan. I'm sorry. I didn't mean to steal your bed for the night. Where did you sleep?"

"I set up my cot in front of the fireplace. It's quite cozy right by the rug. I can see why Suzie likes it so much." Dugan gave her a broad smile, looking fully refreshed. *Apparently, he didn't work through the night again but came right back and just let Goldilocks continue to sleep in his bed.*

He set down the staple gun and walked over to his kitchenette. He picked up two bowls. "I made you something for breakfast. It won't be anything like your meals, but I thought you might wake up hungry. You fell asleep so early yesterday that I don't even know if you ate a proper meal."

He handed her a bowl and a spoon and sat on the edge of his bed, so Gina did the same, even though there was a small table just a few yards across the room. It was almost like he could read her mind, and she stared at the formless porridge in front of her. "This is perfect. Thank you. I'm starving."

Dugan took her bowl when she finished. "So, I know you like your independence, and that's something I can appreciate, but I worry about you crawling in and out of that window of the fallen treehouse with those stitches. I'm sorry if I sound like a mimic bird, but I just want to make sure you know you're welcome to stay here if you want."

Gina thought about the amazing sleep she got last night and how refreshed she already felt. "All right, I'll stay for a few days. But just until my stitches are better."

Chapter 18

Goldilocks

G ina

The next day, Gina looked around the kitchen of Nathan's compound and gave a gigantic sigh of relief. Finally. The kitchen was all repaired and cleaned. Gina listened to the banging from upstairs. After fixing the kitchen, there were now three men fixing up the roof of Brianna's old room. Hopefully, they would finish today and be able to start on the employee housing tomorrow when the rest of their crew arrived.

Dugan was working his hardest to clean up the island, but he was stressing so much about getting everything ready. *Nathan seemed nice enough at the interview. It must have been that accident that happened with a smuggler that's making Dugan paranoid that everything has to be perfect before the Riley family returns.*

She whipped together lunch for herself, Dugan, Thomas, Tim, and his small construction crew. She still didn't have the supplies to make anything fancy but had salvaged enough to feed all the hardworking, hungry men. Thomas had promised to bring her a large load of groceries tomorrow when he brought the animals back.

Gina used canned chicken gravy, canned chicken, and canned veg-etables to make a pot pie mix. She found flour in an airtight container in the pantry that she used to make a basic biscuit. She added seasoning but frowned at the results. These were not the nice fancy meals she'd planned on making here to impress her new employers. Even though the employees knew she was short on supplies, she didn't want to disappoint them with the basic food she could come up with.

Gina finished lunch and packed everything up into containers. She took three servings upstairs for Tim's construction crew. They were overly grateful and gracious. They looked at her meager meal hungrily and thanked her for taking the time to make them something.

Salivating over the delicious smells, Gina ate her own meal before packing up the last two servings into a basket. She'd spent the last day and a half staying close to the compound because of her stitches but was now feeling claustrophobic. It would be so nice to take a long walk and stretch her legs before she had to come back and start dinner. She would go slowly and stick to the path, and she was sure she would be fine. She started out heading toward the secret garden to take Thomas his meal.

Dugan could have been anywhere on the island. Hopefully, she would run into him on her way there or back. If not, she would just bring it back and put it in the fridge for later. It wasn't like her beast master wasn't used to taking care of himself.

Gina stepped out into the warm, beautiful day. The jungle gave off a slight mist to cool her, but not enough to be uncomfortable. It impressed her; the paths were already looking pretty clear. *That poor man must work until he is ready to drop.*

"Dugan! Pongo! Suzie!" Gina called out. If the dogs were nearby, she hoped they would hear her. She heard no response, so she continued. She spotted a beautiful large pink flower. On a whim, she picked it up and tucked it behind her ear. She felt so safe and almost whimsical there. This was a place Maxwell couldn't reach her.

Eventually, she reached the secret garden. She carefully crossed the bridge that Thomas had fixed that led across the moat, making sure to only walk on the outer boards and not get dumped into the dark water below. The main door of the secret garden was ajar, so Gina walked in.

The garden looked all cleaned up. Someone had piled loose sticks in the corner, and a hole in the greenhouse looked patched. Lots of rotted and ruined vegetables were piled high into a heap, but some plants had survived. There were stakes in the ground tied to a few sad looking plants that were trying to recover from being blown around so much by the wind.

Thomas was shirtless, bent over the chicken hutch, drilling something in. She observed him working for a few moments. The muscles on his back glistened from the sweat of working in the scorching sun. He didn't even realize she was there.

When the drilling stopped, Gina cleared her throat. "Thomas, I brought you some lunch."

In surprise, Thomas whipped around and spotted her. The biggest smile grew on his face, and he got up and walked over to a water pump. "That is the kindest thing, Gina. I'm starving. I really appreciate it, but you didn't have to come all the way out here to feed me. You're injured and I'm sure you have plenty of other things to do."

Thomas used his hands to cup water from the pump and splash it over his face and chest. Then he picked up his shirt that was hanging on a post nearby and pulled it on. The shirt clung to his body where it was still wet.

Gina's face turned pink at the praise. "I know I didn't have to. I was feeling very accomplished when I finished cleaning up the kitchen and needed to go for a walk. Unfortunately, I don't have any fresh supplies, so what I can make is basic. If you don't want it, it's no big deal. I can always take it back and stick it in the fridge."

Thomas put his hand to his chest and opened his eyes wide in mock worry. "Please don't take it away! Whatever you brought smells delicious from here. Believe me, it's better than the rations I brought for myself for the next few days. I didn't want to bring anything that needed refrigerating because I didn't know the state I would find things in here. Thank you. I really appreciate you thinking of me."

Gina got out the containers and handed them over. "Do you have any idea where Dugan might be? I also have food for him too."

Thomas looked thoughtful. "I believe he said he was going to clear out the area where the new employee housing is going. I'm leaving shortly to bring in some basic building supplies tomorrow on my ark of animals, and he wanted to have everything ready so the construction crew could get right to work preparing the ground for cement."

Thomas smiled and pointed around to the different areas of the garden. "What do you think? It's looking pretty good, right? I think the animals will be happy to return home and get settled back in."

Gina smiled. "Yes, I'm sure they will be thrilled. It seems like you will be too by the way you speak of them. Well, I had better be off to find Dugan. With the way he has been working, he won't stop to eat unless I make him."

Thomas sat on a bench overlooking the garden and opened up his containers. He took a big bite of the biscuit. "This is delicious. Is there honey in this?"

Gina nodded shyly. "Yes. I hope you enjoy it. If you need help to get all the animals out here tomorrow, come and get me."

Thomas nodded because his mouth was too full to reply. With a happy heart, Gina turned and walked out of the garden. *It will be so nice when I can come here to collect fresh eggs and vegetables for the dinners I make. The Rileys are in for a treat!*

A slight ache throbbed where her stitches were, but Gina ignored it. It couldn't be that much farther to deliver Dugan's lunch. After all the kindness he'd shown her, it was the least she could do for him.

She reached the area where the employee housing was to be built. She spotted Dugan's broad shoulders wielding a chainsaw and a gigantic pile of logs piled up on the edge of the clearing he was widening. Gina's side was throbbing painfully by this point, so she sat on a log and watched him work until he took a break. It wasn't long before he cut a huge log off the base of a downed tree. It was half the size of Dugan, but the man easily rolled it over to where Gina sat.

She held up the basket she had brought with her. "I brought you lunch."

Dugan gave her an enormous grin. "Thank you. I'm so hungry, I could eat a rhinoceros right now."

Gina chuckled at his sayings, wondering where he picked them up. "Well, I hope you enjoy. I need to get back and start dinner in a few hours if you want to come and join me; I would appreciate the company."

Dugan took the basket and peered inside while he nodded his head vigorously. "Yes, I would love to join you."

Gina stood up and winced at the pain that shot through her side. Dugan must have noticed her discomfort because he dropped the basket and was immediately at her side. "Gina, you're bleeding through your shirt. You've been overdoing things, haven't you? Do you mind if I look to make sure you don't need restitching?"

Gina lifted her shirt that was sticky with blood in one spot. Dugan got down on his knee and examined it so closely that she could feel his breath on her skin. "How does it look?"

He gently ran a finger around the area. "The stitches are holding for now, but it is bleeding and the skin around your wound is looking pink. Why don't you go back to my cottage and get some antiseptic for it and lay down for a bit."

An argument about how she was fine came to Gina's lips, but she was in too much pain to express them, so she simply nodded. Dugan gave a sigh of relief and wrapped an arm around her to help support her. "Come on. I'll walk you back."

They shambled on together a few feet until Dugan swung her up into his arms and started walking much more quickly back to his cottage. Gina let out a surprised squeal, but Dugan headed off any arguments. "Let me carry you. I know you can make it back yourself, but this way primes my muscles for carrying more logs."

Gina relaxed against his chest since it seemed easier for him when he was carrying her instead of leaning over trying to help her limp. She looked up into his face and wondered if he felt more between them than just friendship like she did. A part of her hoped so, but another part was terrified.

Chapter 19

Don't Run Away, Take a Muffin!

Dugan

A few days later, Dugan woke to the smell of freshly baked muffins wafting through his cottage. Gina was busy in his kitchenette whipping something up for breakfast, and it was a sight to see. One he wanted to see every day for the rest of his life. Too bad she'd made it abundantly clear that she was feeling well enough to move back into her treehouse tomorrow. He was going to miss having her around and waking in the night to see her sprawled out across his entire bed.

He walked over to the small kitchen table and sat down, rubbing the sleepers out of his eye. Gina sat down across from him and placed two cups of coffee on the table. She peered over her mug at Dugan. Chee Chee settled on his shoulder, eating a nut for his breakfast. Dugan took a large gulp of coffee as Gina started the conversation. "Please tell me you aren't planning on directing Tim and his construction crew by pointing to a pile of land and saying build there."

Dugan's eyebrow rose in confusion. "What else do I need to say, exactly? They have the blueprints."

Gina gave an exasperated sigh. "I know you think the manly thing to do is to grunt and everything will work out. Unfortunately, these people you have coming to the island need more direction than that. They need to know the details, such as where they're going to sleep tonight, what they're going to eat, and how they are going to get supplies for their job. I've been cooking for everyone here, so the three construction guys keep coming to me with all of their questions. You need to talk to them."

Dugan smiled at her, trying to turn his grogginess into something resembling charm. "I don't know. I think it's working out great. You're much prettier to talk to than those guys. Maybe I want a reason for you to seek me out."

Gina frowned, then changed the subject. "Well, you'd better get moving. Tim is finishing up the upstairs at Nathan's compound, and he said the rest of his construction crew should be here around eight. This island can be… a little intimidating. I think it would be nice if you welcomed them."

Gina pulled out a basket and placed a few extra blueberry muffins she'd made from a pre-made mix in the pantry. She placed them in the basket and covered it with a thin linen cloth to keep them fresh. She set the basket down in front of Dugan. "Here, you can take them these. That should make them feel welcome."

Dugan looked at the basket but didn't touch it. Bringing baked goods to people really wasn't his style, but if it would make Gina happy, he would do it. He was becoming way too fond of that beautiful woman and becoming too dependent on her as well. He didn't think he would be able to on-board these new employees without her support. Especially with the limited resources and massive amounts of work he was trying to accomplish in the meantime.

Dugan walked outside and whistled. Suzie and Pongo came running out of the woods immediately. Both stopped at his sides and waited patiently for instruction. Dugan smiled and petted both of their heads. Pongo was coming along well in his training. *Looks like it's time to invite the security staff to the island and find Pongo his new partner.*

Dugan continued down the path toward the docks. When he reached the area where the weeds were fighting for dominance, he directed the dogs to spread out. He quietly spoke to Chee Chee. He may have feigned annoyance at the small animal's antics, but he was really growing quite fond of the little guy. "Hold on, little buddy."

He pulled out a machete that he kept on his belt and whacked at the plants near the edge of the path, weed and flower alike. He needed to get this island cleared out before Nathan returned. He wanted Nathan to feel comfortable when he came home, not like he was returning to a war zone.

When Dugan reached the docks, he spotted an empty boat tied up. He was glad it was holding up well. It needed to be in tiptop shape for when Thomas brought the farm animals back tonight.

Curiously, Dugan looked around the nearby jungle, trying to determine where the men had gone. He heard barking. It was Suzie.

Swiftly, he moved toward the sound. They huddled together, four men in jeans and stained, paint-covered clothes.

Pongo stood guard on one side of them and Suzie stood on the other, so the men had no escape. Dugan firmly called out, "Heel." Both dogs immediately dropped back and stood beside Dugan.

One man had a wet spot on his pants. Apparently, the dogs had given him a bit of a fright. Another man bent down and struggled with the noose around his foot. *Oops, missed one.*

Dugan told the dogs to stay and approached the men with one hand up in peace and the other still gripping the basket of muffins. "Here, let me help you with that. My name is Dugan. I'm head of security here on the island. Once we get you out of this, I can take you to the main work area. Tim is waiting for you there."

The man with the stain on his pants looked on wide-eyed and backed up with every step that Dugan took forward. "No, thank you. I'm not staying on this crazy island. This place is a death trap. I should have never agreed to come."

He looked over at his comrades. "You guys should leave with me. This is like the beginning of a horror movie. Believe me, if you stay, you won't survive the night."

Dugan reached for the man whose foot was stuck. "There is no need for that. There's nothing on this island that will hurt you." He knelt and loosened it. As soon as his foot was free, the man scurried out of the way.

He looked around at the others uneasily. "I don't know. It is rumored that this island is covered in traps and puzzles. Tourists that come out here never return." He pointed at Suzie, who stood watching him intently, ready to jump to Dugan's aid at a moment's notice if necessary.

"I mean, look at the size of that dog. It could eat me for dinner." He pointed to the one man that was small and scrawny. "You will be dessert. I'm leaving." The other two men nodded their heads in agreement.

Dugan looked at the men speechlessly. He needed these men if he wanted to keep to his timeline. He was so bad with people. What would Gina do in this situation? Totally out of character, Dugan raised the basket of muffins in the air, plastered on his best fake smile, and said, "I brought muffins. Have one, and I'll show you around. You will see it isn't so bad."

The men looked back and forth at each other. One man even seemed to shake a bit. "Nope, we're out. Sorry, man." The men gave the dogs a wide berth as they swiftly walked and then ran past Dugan back to the docks.

Dugan groaned. *What am I going to do now?* There was no way he could get the new employee housing built in time without those extra men. Stress and anxiety coursed through his body as he tried to think about how he could pull this project off without letting Nathan down. Dugan pulled out a muffin that was still slightly warm from the oven and took a large bite. *At least this leaves more of Gina's muffins for me.*

Chapter 20

Off the Ark

G^{ina}

Later that afternoon, Gina waited down at the docks for Thomas to bring in the animals. She moved around experimentally and smiled with the satisfaction that she was almost healed now and was present to help like she promised. She saw a longboat enter the cove with Thomas at the helm.

After he tied up the boat, Thomas jumped off onto the dock. "Hey, Gina! Thanks for giving me a hand. It's a lot of effort getting these guys to the secret garden, and fewer trips will make all the difference for me. Are you ready to meet Bingo?"

Gina nodded. *Was Bingo a chicken name?* Soon Thomas led a large brown-and-white animal by a tether slowly off the boat and onto the shore. Gina followed until he handed her the lead. "This is Bingo the llama." Then he went back to the boat, unloading a handful of crates full of chickens. He walked up to her. "Are you good? Just take Bingo to the garden, and we will keep making trips until my 'ark' is empty."

"Surely I can make it down a pathway with a llama. Let's go." Thomas led the way with the chickens and soon she couldn't see him around a bend. She looked up at her charge, and the llama eyed her back.

Bingo munched on a few small green leaves while Gina gently yanked on the rope tied around his neck. She ground her teeth as she yanked again. "Come on, Bingo! At this rate, we will take all day getting to the secret garden. Thomas has food for you there. Do you want to go to the secret garden and get some yummy food?"

Still chewing, Bingo slowly turned his head and looked at her with a bland, almost bored expression. He went back to chewing until Gina's insistent yanks convinced him to take a few more steps down the trail.

When she had offered to help Thomas bring the animals ashore, she'd pictured carrying a few crates, not convincing this large, stubborn animal to take another step forward. Pongo came up the pathway, wagging his behind excitedly as he greeted her enthusiastically with his wet tongue. Gina couldn't help smiling at the dog's exuberance.

A few moments later, Dugan came down the path the opposite way she was going and whistled for Pongo to return. "Struggling with Bingo, huh? I see you're trying to be gentle with him, but you have to keep a steady pressure on the rope to keep him going. If you let the rope go lax, he thinks he has time to grab a bite to eat. Try that and you might get him moving faster."

Gina nodded at his advice but left the rope lax for a few more minutes. She couldn't help stepping closer to Dugan's reassuring presence. "Where are you off to in such a chipper mood?"

Dugan grinned from ear to ear. "I made some calls and used every persuasive word in my body. There is a boat coming in with my new security crew and a few more guys that will join Tim's construction crew. I even got a hold of the two men who are going to focus solely on doing supply runs. There are a lot of construction materials Tim needs, and we need that kitchen of yours restocked. Are you interested in helping me pick out some basic furniture that we're going to supply for the employee housing?"

Gina beamed up at Dugan. She liked how he was always asking for her opinions and taking her advice. "Sure. I would be happy to help. That means I get to pick out my furniture."

Dugan let out an enormous sigh. His muscles relaxed, and he looked calmer than he had since she met him. "I just feel like everything is coming together. I know we only have five weeks until the Riley family returns, but Tim's men have been doing a great job preparing and laying the foundation for the first employee housing building. If we just focus on that one instead of trying to do both at once, I'm finally feeling like we might make our deadline and have everyone moved out of Nathan's spare bedrooms before he returns. He has been very understanding about letting us stay there, but I still don't want to let him down."

Dugan paused and looked like he wanted to say something else to her, but he looked away. "Well, I'd better get down to the docks, then. Pongo's going to meet his new master soon. This pup still has a lot of learning to do, but he's on the right track. I'm thinking of breeding Suzie one more time to see if I can get one more pup that would have a suitable disposition and intelligence for security work. That would give us three solid human/canine security teams. No one will slip past security again."

As soon as Dugan walked by, she tightened her hold on the rope and directed Bingo farther down the path. It worked.

Eventually, she made it to the secret garden. Thomas was standing amongst a flock of funny-looking fuzzy chickens, throwing mealworms for them. The birds were flapping around excitedly, pecking at the ground.

When Bingo spotted Thomas, he pulled the lead rope loose from Gina's hands and butted his head against the man. Thomas, surprised, fell onto his rump, laughing. His cowboy hat fluttered to the ground for the birds to investigate. "Bingo, my boy! Are you happy to be home? We will have the goats back for you to boss around shortly."

Gina couldn't stop staring as she watched Thomas interact with Bingo. It obviously delighted the animal to be returned to his home with his master. In Bingo's world, everything was as it should be.

The sad thing was, Thomas treated this animal better than Maxwell had ever treated her. He never physically abused her, but he ignored and controlled her. She wondered if she would carry the unseen emotional scars for the rest of her life.

Sure, Maxwell would act like the doting boyfriend in front of others, but as soon as they were alone, he quizzed her on everything she'd said and to whom. He didn't want her to leave his mansion unless he sent one of his men with her.

Thomas brought her back to the present as he got up and walked toward her. Dirt and chicken poop covered his clothing. His cowboy hat was back on his head, but slightly askew. He smiled at her freely. She didn't think there was a mean thought running through that man's bones.

Thomas arched his eyebrow as he asked her, "How did it go bringing Bingo up here? I was just about to go looking for you two, but it looks like you made it."

She didn't want to explain how much trouble she'd had at first, so she said, "It went fine. We made it, didn't we? Although, instead of helping with the goats, on the next load I was hoping I could take some of the kitchen supplies to the compound. I'm dying to get my hands on all the goodies you brought, and I am hoping to make everyone a proper meal for dinner to celebrate."

Thomas stepped toward her. "You know, you look cute when you're excited about your kitchen. What are we celebrating?"

"We are celebrating how everything is coming together on this island and how it's already feeling like home."

Chapter 21

Trying to be Friendly

D^{ugan}

Dugan waved a hand at the group of men and women pulling their boat up to the dock. Pongo stood beside him, shaking his tail excitedly, ready to greet the newcomers. Suzie sat more sedately, her eyes watching both her pup and the arriving boat. He tried his best to give a cheery greeting, but all he really wanted to do was go back down the path and help Gina get Bingo to the secret garden.

He pictured in his head helping her down the path and her smiling up at him gratefully. She would comment on how strong and good with animals he was, and maybe he would be brave enough to tell her how good she was for him.

That intriguing woman sure caught his attention, and he didn't think he would ever be the same since meeting her. Right then, instead of getting down to business and preparing to on-board his new employees, he was mooning after a woman who would never see a big brute like himself as more than a coworker.

When the crew finally docked, one man threw him a rope. He used a thick cord to tie up to the dock, and the people stepped off the boat, some expertly, some awkwardly. The first man to jump to the dock walked over to Dugan with his hand outstretched.

His short brown hair moved in the breeze, and his skin was as tan as the wet sand below the dock. "Hello. My name's Keith. This is my boat, the Chainsaw." He glanced over his shoulder and pointed to a man in a red shirt who was still on the boat. "That is my crewmate, Terrance."

Dugan nodded. "Thanks so much for dropping off these folks for us. It's going to be a lot easier on me having you ferry people back and forth on your weekly visits."

Digging in his pocket, Dugan pulled out a long list he had compiled. "Here is the list of all the construction materials, animal feed, and kitchen supplies we should need for next week. Hopefully, our supply lists will get more regular once Riley's Paradise Island is full of Rileys again. Right now, we are making a lot of changes and figuring out exactly what we need."

Keith took the list from Dugan and glanced over it. "All right. We will bring these to you. Same place, same time next week. I'll give you a call if I have any questions. Looking forward to working with you."

Unsure what to say to the man next, Dugan blurted out, "Did you guys want to stay for dinner? Our cook, Gina, will be making something delicious in a few hours."

Keith shrugged. "I have nothing going on. It will just be me and my boat on a moonlit pizza date otherwise." He turned to Terrance and spoke loudly enough that he could be heard a few yards away. "How about you, Terrance? Want to stay for a few hours?"

Terrance shook his head and shouted back, "No. The wife will have my hide if I'm not back for dinner. She's usually at her wits' end by the evening."

Keith frowned and turned back to Dugan. "Terrance has five kids under six. I'll take you up on that offer another time, then. Have a good afternoon."

"Thanks again," Dugan replied as Keith and Terrance walked back to the boat, untied the rope, and started motoring off out of the bay.

They left a group of three men and two women standing on the dock. They were a younger group, all in their mid-twenties. They shifted around nervously, looking into the jungle. One man and one woman had backpacking gear that they hoisted back onto their backs after getting off the boat. The woman in particular seemed to take a fancy to Pongo. She knelt down and was petting the dog enthusiastically.

Dugan greeted the group of young people first. He didn't want to lose another group of nervous employees to the rumored stories they were told on the mainland. "Hello, my name is Dugan. I'm head of security on Riley's Paradise Island. This is a great place to live, and the Rileys are a pleasure to work for. I look forward to getting to know and work with each one of you."

He got a few reassuring smiles from the group, so he pushed on. He looked directly at the two individuals with backpacks. "You two must be my new security team, Susan and Buck. It looks like you guys brought camping supplies like I directed. Good work. You two will spend the next few weeks camping out around the island to get to know every part of this place intimately."

The young woman patted Pongo another time before looking at him. "Sir, are the rumors true? Are there really traps and riddles all over this island to catch trespassing vacationers?"

Dugan replied, "Like a bird trying to hold two berries in its beak, those rumors are both true and they are not. As you will soon see, there are traps and riddles all over the island, but we do not design them for vacationers. Originally, the brothers, Nathan and Jackson set some of them up as games, but over time they have morphed into a part of the defensive strategy for the island security."

Dugan pointed out some of the easily visible trees strewn about in the nearby jungle. "The storm disabled most of the traps, some of them permanently and some temporarily. It will be our job to fix and maintain them, but in the meantime, we will have to be on our guard even more. More than once, people up to no good have made their way onto this remote island. I will give you a rundown of the place and get you settled in temporary rooms until the employee housing is complete."

Turning to the other man and woman, Dugan noted that they'd each brought their own duffel bags. "Thank you for coming to help us build our new employee housing. I wanted to let you know that after a call with Nathan, our boss, he said that we will make the island a lot more family-friendly. So, while I imagine the island will always hold many puzzles and unique challenges, you have nothing to fear here. It will be safe. Come with me, and I'll take you two to meet Tim, your foreman."

Dugan led the four people down the path, feeling very crowded on his usually empty island. All these people about would certainly take some getting used to. He figured he would drop off the rest of the construction crew with Tim first, so at least he only had two people that he needed to take care of. Having employees was already exhausting.

Peering around every bend, Dugan couldn't help hoping that Gina hadn't made it to the secret garden yet. Bingo was as stubborn as they came. She could be right up ahead, and he could swoop in and help her. He was quite disappointed when he didn't run into her on the path again.

Chapter 22

Dreading the Rileys

G^{ina}

Gina looked around at the faces sitting around the kitchen table, enthusiastically munching on the dinner she'd made for them. In the last five weeks, these people had become her family. People she could laugh and joke with. People she felt comfortable around, who respected her. Her new family.

In a way, she dreaded the Rileys coming back to their island next week. The employees had developed a routine and learned to work together. She didn't know exactly how her days would soon look, but they definitely would never be the same.

Glancing to her right, Gina saw Dugan. His calm presence always seemed to be beside her at these impromptu gatherings. He placed one of his enormous hands over hers, encompassing their entirety. He ducked his head down to look her in the eye, and she saw what looked like compassion and concern. "What's wrong, Gina? Dinner is delicious. I don't think I have ever had a shrimp florentine that melts in my mouth like this. Why aren't you eating?"

Gina twirled her fork around in her pasta. Her earlier thoughts of upcoming change had made her lose her appetite. She gave a heavy sigh before responding, "I've just come to look forward to this time with everyone. I guess I'm kind of afraid of all of us being too busy to have time to sit down like this once the Rileys arrive."

Dugan grinned and raised his eyebrows in mock shock. "This coming from the woman who stubbornly sleeps in a fallen-down treehouse every night? The woman who spent the first few days we were together scowling at me like I was invading her own personal island?"

Gina pursed her lips together. He had her pegged. A lot had changed over the last few weeks. She felt like the good company and hard work had healed something in her she didn't even realize was broken. "I guess you... I mean, you guys have grown on me."

A flash of surprise crossed Dugan's face when he heard her slip, but he masked it so fast that she didn't know what to make of it. Dugan said, "Don't worry. Between the two employee housing buildings, there is going to be a common building. It will have some tables, a kitchenette, a pool table, couches, and a television. We can still make this a regular thing, even if it won't be as frequent."

Tim cleared his throat from across the table. Everyone's heads turned toward him as he stood up. He held up his glass of water. "Gina, we all have really appreciated you cooking for us and helping us find our way here. We understand it isn't your job and you will be too busy cooking for the Rileys soon, so we just wanted to let you know how much we appreciate you. In fact, my crew and I have a surprise waiting for you at the first employee housing building we are working on. Would you like to go for a stroll to see?"

Tears filled Gina's eyes as she tried to will them into not falling and embarrassing her. Dugan had the largest grin on his face and was uncharacteristically shifting around from one foot to the other in excitement. *He must be in on this too.* "All right, let me clean up from dinner..."

Susan and Buck quickly interrupted her. "Don't worry, we will clean up tonight. You can go ahead."

Gina looked at the group suspiciously. She took a few seconds to study each face around her, looking for clues about the surprise. Her eyes ended on Dugan's kindhearted face. She couldn't believe how such a giant man could make her feel so safe when an innocuous-looking one had made her life a living hell.

Resigning herself to their mercies, she finally felt better enough to take a bite to eat. "After dessert at least?" Not one sole argued with that.

***

Gina walked up to the building Tim and his construction crew had been working on nonstop for the last few weeks. Only Dugan had come with her. Everyone else made excuses for why they needed to stay back. From the outside, it looked complete, but when she'd walked in the front door a few days ago, the place still needed an enormous amount of work.

There had been electrical wires hanging out of walls and plumbing that led to nowhere. They'd piled insulation and drywall around in giant mounds, and the furniture that just came in filled the framing of one apartment.

The men and women working on it had been proud to show off their progress in such a short term. It was an impressive amount of work that they had accomplished, but from what she saw, she was worried they wouldn't have things ready for when the Rileys arrived back on their paradise island, expecting the employees to be out of their house.

She took a deep breath before walking in the front door. She was expecting things to look the same. *Did Keith bring a present in from the mainland when he dropped off supplies last time?*

She walked through the front door and nodded her head to show it impressed her that the team had accomplished so much. There was drywall up, forming the outline of most of the rooms, and fluffy pink insulation poking out from the edges of the parts that were to be completed next.

Dugan watched her intently as she studied the rooms. "I don't know if Tim explained the vision here, but there are going to be two studio apartments on this first floor, two studio apartments on the second floor, and a small family apartment on the third floor. Each will have a private bathroom and kitchenette. The second employee housing apartment will be identical, with a small building between the two to act as a common area, with its own kitchen, dining area, large-screen television, and laundry facilities."

She nodded in approval. Tim had explained most of that to her, and the goal was to only have the first employee housing building built before the Rileys returned, but she couldn't help the knot in her stomach. Of course, if they could get the major construction finished, they could always do the finishing touches with the employees staying there.

Dugan gently reached for her hand and pulled her toward the stairs. "Come on. Your surprise is up here." Her face turned slightly pink at his touch, even though there was nothing romantic about his touch or their surroundings. To her surprise, he didn't let her go until they were on the second floor.

The second floor held two smaller apartments, but only one had a door attached. She glanced into the apartment on the left to see that it was mostly bare walls they were starting to mud. Dugan curled a lip as he told her, "Thomas insisted the apartment across from yours is going to be his." *Is he displeased with Thomas for picking an apartment? He seems nice enough, and Dugan has his own cottage.*

His lip evened back out as he continued explaining the plans for the rest of the housing. "The construction crew and security personnel will share the other apartments temporarily until they have completed enough apartments for all the permanent employees to have their own housing."

Slightly worried, Gina asked, "What do you mean by 'the permanent employees?'"

He shrugged. "You, me, and my extra security hires Nathan plans on keeping. They only hired the construction crew temporarily, and they will leave after the employee housing and Walter and Jackson's house is finished. After the construction is complete, Nathan plans on hiring a housekeeper to take care of the cleaning at his compound, and Walter will probably hire his own housekeeper/cook. He would also like to keep a maintenance man that can fix housing and traps and be able to do minor construction projects as needed."

Dugan opened the door on the right. "It almost feels like we are building a little community here on the island." Gina followed close behind him, curious about her surprise.

She gasped as she saw a small perfectly painted apartment, with beautiful wood flooring and large windows overlooking the jungle. She stepped inside to see the simple furniture she had helped pick out laid out just as she imagined it. There was a kitchenette that had a small table with two chairs. The bathroom had the gray linens and shower curtain she helped Dugan pick out from a magazine. The bedroom had a queen-sized bed with a headboard that matched the dresser next to it.

Gina turned to Dugan. "Wow, this is even more perfect than I imagined. You guys outdid yourselves! I'm glad you showed me so I can look forward to what my apartment will look like soon. Who is the lucky person to get this one?"

Dugan took both of her hands in his own and looked deeply into her eyes. "Gina. This is yours. You have worked so hard for the rest of us that we thought the least we could do was get you a decent place to sleep. Mind you, there will be a lot of banging and construction in other parts of this building for the next few weeks still, but this is yours."

Tears streamed down Gina's face, and she surprised herself as she stood on her tiptoes and gave Dugan a short but sweet peck of a kiss on his cheek. A jolt of electricity shot from her lips to the core of her body, making her curious about what his lips would feel like against her own. She immediately backed away and tried to get a hold of herself.

"Dugan, this was the nicest thing anyone has ever done for me. This means the world to me, and I don't know how I can ever repay you. Thank you." A home all to herself. A place to belong where she could be the person she wanted to be. This place really was her refuge.

Dugan's cheeks turned pink as he looked away and mumbled, "You know, it wasn't all me, although I helped to get the painting done."

She smiled up at the large man and turned away, opening cabinets and examining every inch of her new space. "I will have to make an extra-special meal for everyone tomorrow to say thank you." If only she could figure out how to squash these burgeoning feelings for Dugan, everything would be perfect.

Chapter 23

Rileys Back in Town

G^{ina}

The voice of a little girl carried down the hallways. "I'm home! I'm home! It's so good to be home!"

Sounds like the Rileys are here.

Dugan had told her to expect Nathan, Brianna, and their little girl, Jenna, today but hadn't known what time they would arrive. She was ready to prepare a snack or a meal in a hurry, depending on what time they arrived.

She opened the refrigerator and quickly pulled out the biscuit dough and cookie batter to prepare for the oven. Once it was cooking, she would put the final touches on her charcuterie board and fruit salad. She wanted something ready for them as soon as they settled themselves, and she wanted to make a good first impression.

Roughly twenty minutes later, she pulled the cookies out to cool. She turned around and spotted a small blond-haired girl staring at her from the doorway. The little girl frowned and said, "You're not Debbie."

Gina tried to give the little girl her most encouraging smile. Luckily, Dugan had told her how Debbie used to cook for Nathan twice a week and for his brother and father once a week until Nathan had hired a full-time cook. Her.

Oddly, when the hurricane came through, Nathan's father, Walter, had stayed with Debbie on the mainland instead of joining his sons on a treasure hunt in Scotland. She had a feeling there was more going on there in the romance department but didn't have anything to back it up. Maybe he just really liked Debbie's cooking.

"Your name's Jenna, right?" The little girl nodded. "You will have to ask your dad what Debbie is doing now. I can't answer that, but I can tell you about myself. My name is Gina, and I am your new cook. I can't wait to hear about all of your favorite foods so I can make them especially for you."

A woman with sandy-brown hair walked up to the kitchen door and gave the little girl a one-armed hug. "Jenna, there you are. I should have guessed that you would follow the scent of cookies."

The woman looked up at Gina and walked into the kitchen with her hand extended. Gina noticed her tummy extended slightly under her shirt. It was large enough to make Gina wonder if she was pregnant, but small enough that it could've been a little extra weight.

The woman wore a bright smile as she shook Gina's hand vigorous-ly. "Hello. I'm Brianna, and you must be our new cook. I can't believe you have this ready. It looks delicious!"

Gina's cheeks turned pink at the praise, and she gestured toward the counter filled with food. She'd always loved to cook, but it was only in the past few weeks that she realized how satisfying it was to cook for a thankful crowd. "Yes, you can help yourselves. I didn't know if you would be hungry from your travels, so I prepared a little something, just in case."

Brianna grabbed two plates, gestured for Jenna to join her, and started filling them as she continued talking. "I'm famished. The only things in the world I want right now are to eat some of this delicious food and take a long nap! After Scotland, we went and visited Nathan's ailing aunt. It was good that we visited. She needed Nathan's help to settle her estate, but it was emotionally exhausting."

Fiddling with her hands, Gina didn't know what to do with herself now that the food was served. When she was serving the other employees, she would just make herself a plate and sit to join everyone. This was a different dynamic and would take some getting used to.

"When you are feeling more rested, if you want to let me know what some of your family's favorite meals are, I can have the supplies delivered next week. I tried to have Dugan help me prepare for the meals this week, but most of his comments weren't all that helpful. I believe he said that you guys liked to eat 'pasta with green stuff on it and chicken that tastes superb.'"

Brianna laughed. "Yes, I can see him being too busy over the last year trying to keep this island running to have a clue what Nathan and I were eating. I'll fill you in on the things we like, but we also like to try new things, so you can be creative."

Gina watched as Brianna led Jenna to the table in the kitchen instead of leaving for the formal dining room. Gina had stressed over deciding where to serve the finished snack. She had finally left it in the kitchen because it would be easier to take it into the dining room than to bring it back into the kitchen. At least for informal snacks, it looked like the kitchen was the winner.

While washing dishes, Gina spotted Nathan entering the kitchen. "There are my lovely ladies." He was still the same handsome man that interviewed her months ago, but today he looked a lot more tired. He walked over to the kitchen table, gave Jenna a kiss on the head, gave Brianna a kiss on the lips, and stroked her belly.

I guess she is pregnant. I should have some ginger tea and different crackers on hand in case she has morning sickness. How in the world do I prepare for weird food cravings on a remote island? I can't exactly fill the fridge with pickles and ice cream.

After greeting his wife and daughter, he came over to the food and started making himself a plate. He was piling it so high that she was afraid something would roll off. "Gina, you have outdone yourself. Thank you so much for this delicious-looking spread. Fresh cookies? You didn't even know exactly what time we would get back today. I'm impressed."

Gina was interrupted from having to give an embarrassing response by Jenna. She finished her cookie and was looking at her father, almost in tears. "Daddy, where is Debbie? I miss Debbie days, and I don't want her to go away. I love her."

Nathan gave her a reassuring smile. "Well, Little... I mean, Jenna. I have exciting news for you. Your grandfather asked Debbie to marry him. They are coming to stay with us in our house in a few days since the storm messed up your grandfather's house. Debbie is going to be your new grandmother."

Chapter 24

Cowardly Lion

D

I've only known her for about two months, but every day, I can't stop thinking about her, and every night, I can't stop dreaming about her. How do I get Gina out of my head? It's painful that she will never be mine, but do I really want her out of my mind?

Dugan finally decided. He was going to stop being so passive. Gina seemed to enjoy his company, and honestly, he didn't think he could stay on this island, seeing her every day and never being anything more than friends.

Thinking back to his last genuine relationship, he groaned inwardly at his awkward teenager years. He'd gone to a small country school with only one hundred and three kids in his graduating class. He did date a girl, the pastor's daughter, but it never went beyond a few kisses. Then he joined the military, where he had a few one-night stands to blow off some steam, but nothing serious.

After he came home, everything just seemed so hard. He tried to date, but he needed a lot of quiet and solitude. Most women didn't understand and thought he was ghosting them when he took some time to himself to recharge. He was a nervous wreck when he tried to go to loud busy places like concerts or even busy restaurants, and that made it very difficult to date.

When he'd met Nathan and he offered him a job on Riley's Paradise Island, it was like a dream come true. Suzie was all the partner he wanted. He could have all the peace he needed, and he hadn't missed the companionship of women until now.

Dugan's palms grew sweaty at the thought of inviting her on a date, but this amazing woman deserved the best. He would force himself to go out of his comfort if it meant he could win the heart of Gina.

She hadn't left this island in almost two months since she first arrived. Maybe he should invite her to go to the mainland with him. Although, would she consider it romantic if he turned into a nervous wreck? *What if we go shopping and I buy her a nice trinket and do something quieter, like a picnic on the beach? Is that something women like to do in real life or just in the movies?*

Dugan started on his way to second breakfast. At least, that was what Gina had called the time the employees ate. She served the Rileys first breakfast, and then any employees that wanted something to eat showed up for second breakfast. The dynamics of the island were changing, and even the Rileys must have noticed because they ate their meals in the previously unused formal dining room. The nice thing about this change was that it left the kitchen open for whatever employees wanted some of the extra food that Gina regularly cooked, with the Rileys' blessing.

Jackson, Nathan's brother, and Walter, his father, had returned to the island a few days ago. Since the storm had demolished their home, they were staying in Nathan's compound for the time being. Debbie, Nathan's former housekeeper and Walter's new fiancée, would join them shortly after she got her house ready to sell.

It was such a full house, and there were so many employees now that the whole feel of the island had changed. Yes, it still had a lot of its quirky puzzles, but instead of going days without saying a word to anyone but Nathan, now he felt like he had an entire community to watch over. Sometimes it was very nerve-wracking and sometimes it was nice.

Walking into the kitchen with Suzie at his side, his mouth went dry at the sight of Gina. She was whirling about with a bit of flour smudged on her face and a few curls escaping the bun she'd put her hair into. She was beautiful.

He wanted to ask her on a date right then and there, but he paused. What if she said no? At the table, Tim, the head of construction, and Susan, one of his security personnel, sat joking over their breakfast. Dugan nodded his head in approval at Pongo, who lay perfectly still at her feet.

He would ask Gina, but he couldn't get turned down in front of them. It would be too humiliating. Besides, she looked too busy. He probably shouldn't bother her, anyway. He would find the perfect time to ask her on a date later.

Happy with his excuses, Dugan moved toward the plates to fill one for himself. Gina spotted him, giving him the brightest smile. "Dugan! You're here!" It made his heart happy to see such unfettered joy in her eyes. While still beautiful, he remembered the stubborn, standoffish woman he first met trying to live here all by herself. The relaxed woman in front of him had come a long way.

Gina handed a plate to Dugan, but he almost dropped it as she moved to grab a pair of tongs before making sure he had securely taken hold of his dish. "I'm so glad you're here. I tried to make a few too many things this morning, and it's gotten a bit out of hand. Do you mind delivering these to the buffet in the dining room?"

Dugan looked down at the small cheese-stuffed pastries in his hands. He didn't want to say no to her, ever. She didn't know it, but his life was already revolving around the times when he would get to be with her. He made excuses to be in the kitchen multiple times a day, when previously, he would go days without stepping foot in the room since he had his own kitchenette in his cottage.

Mildly, Dugan smiled at her and simply said, "Sure. Anything to help you out." He would never be a man of many words, but what he said, he wanted to share with only one person. He took the pastries into the dining room. Nathan was in a corner of the room talking on his cellphone while Brianna sat in a chair eating saltines and drinking ginger ale. Chee Chee sat on her shoulder, enjoying his own cracker.

Jenna was zooming around the room like an airplane. She almost ran into him, but luckily, he kept Gina's pastries from having a mishap.

"Guess what, Dugan! Tomorrow is Debbie Day! Debbie is coming back to the island, and she's going to be my new grandma!"

Dugan smiled at the small girl. "I heard. I'm sure she will be just as excited to see you." Finally placing the tray on the buffet, Jackson Riley swung by and snagged two pastries to add to his plate that was fifty percent bacon. He didn't see any sign of Mr. Walter Riley. Maybe he was still asleep or out for a morning walk.

After a few minutes, Dugan returned to the kitchen, bringing a few empty dishes with him. Gina sat at the now-empty table with a plate full of food in front of her and another one sitting beside her. Her sweet, soft voice called out to him as he made his way to the sink. "I made you a plate of your favorites if you want to come and join me for second breakfast."

He gently placed the dishes down, washed his hands, and pulled out a chair to join her. "This looks delicious. Thank you so much. I don't think I could go back to eating the dry Army rations I used to have most mornings in my cottage. It seemed so much more efficient to just pop one of those open than bother making an entire meal and having to keep ingredients fresh. I'm getting spoiled."

She took a bite of eggs and washed it down with some tea before responding with a smile. "I'm happy to cook for you forever. I love to cook, and I never realized before I came here how nice it is to cook for appreciative people."

This was it. He had to ask her now before anyone else came into the kitchen. Dugan drank some of the orange juice in front of him and cleared his throat. "So, Gina. I know you haven't had a break from the island in a while, and I was wondering if you wanted to join me for a trip to the mainland."

Gina stiffened, and her fork froze halfway to her mouth. *Does she not want to go with me?* Maybe he shouldn't mention the picnic-on-the-beach idea, and it would sound less like a date. He finished asking her out by lamely adding, "I have to shop for some new boots and thought you would be helpful."

Chapter 25

Professional Boot Shopper

G*ina*

Gina's lip quivered from hurt and confusion. "You need help to go boot shopping?" She had thought Dugan was going to ask her out. The idea of spending time alone with Dugan thrilled her. She was relishing every moment she spent in the large man's presence. He was giving her hope that maybe she had a second chance at love, despite the emotional scars Maxwell had left behind.

Unfortunately, even the thought of leaving her refuge made her stiffen with terror. Here, she was safe. She had a family of friends that liked and respected her. On Riley's Paradise Island, she felt both free and secure. The mainland brought back so many bad feelings and memories.

Memories overwhelmed her senses of sitting at home but not daring to go out because she knew it would upset Maxwell. Suffering through stifling parties where she felt like she was being shown off like a piece of arm candy and then berated when she tried to talk to some gentleman named Jerry he didn't want her to associate with. Everyone thought he was the doting rich, influential boyfriend, and that she was so lucky to get such a great catch, but she knew differently.

It had started so subtly that she didn't even realize how depressed and dependent she had become until she felt there was no escape. That was until she saw an ad to work as a cook on Riley's Paradise Island. She knew it was a long shot because the only genuine work experience she had on her resume was waitressing as a teenager. Of course, Maxwell told her she shouldn't want to work with him supporting her, and she believed him.

Even if her chances were slim, it was worth the risk. She knew Maxwell would make things even worse for her if he found out she applied, and he would have probably taken away the only social outlet she had left, her exercise class at the YMCA. She also knew she had to try.

Now she was on the other side of things and couldn't imagine going back to the way things were. She had to stay away from Maxwell and his overpowering, suffocating presence, no matter the cost. The only question was, what cost was she paying to continue hiding away on her paradise island?

In a way, by not leaving, she was holding herself captive by her fears. To be truly free, she needed to live her life, and she wanted that life to include Dugan, even if they just did something mundane like boot shopping together. It still disappointed her he hadn't asked her out on an actual date, but honestly, maybe going boot shopping was just what she needed. She could focus on something while on the mainland. It was a mission with no strings attached and no stress about where the future would take them. How horrible would it be if she backed out of an actual date? At least this way, she could focus on the simple things, like enjoying her time with Dugan and trying to remember what it felt like to be a normal person in public.

Dugan sat quietly, finishing up his breakfast. Every once in a while, she spotted him stealing glances at her, but after asking her to go boot shopping with him, he had let her take a few minutes to think without saying a word. This man was a real gem. He let her be herself and make her own decisions with no pressure.

Feeling a new resolve, Gina lifted her chin and looked straight into Dugan's captivating blue-green eyes. "You came to the right woman. I happen to be a professional boot shopper."

A half-smile grew on his face as his eyebrow quirked upwards. He looked down at her feet. "A professional boot shopper? How exactly does one get that designation? You know you're wearing sandals, right?"

She grinned back at him, enjoying the easy banter between them. "Did you know that my favorite fairy tale growing up was Puss in Boots? I have spent many hours of my youth drawing short comics of him going on fresh adventures. I always thought I was particularly good at drawing the boots."

Dugan laughed out loud. "That was not the answer I was expecting, but if you can get me a pair of magic boots, then you're hired. Do you still draw? I'd love to see some of your work."

Wistfully, Gina shook her head. "I haven't really felt artistic since... well, for the last few years. Maybe someday I'll start drawing again.

There is certainly enough beauty on this island that it would be a real treat to try to capture some of it on paper. I'll have to think about it."

Gina pursed her lips as she started thinking through the logistics of the trip. "When would you like to go? I would have to check in with Brianna, but if we leave on an upcoming day after breakfast, I can have a cold lunch prepared in the fridge for everyone to help themselves to. Brianna mentioned just the other day that they don't always need to have a big, fancy meal. She said sometimes something simpler would be nice, so they don't gain too much weight from all my cooking. I would just need to be back in time to make dinner."

Dugan finished the last of the meal and stood up and looked down at his boots. Gina looked at them too. They didn't look that old to her, but maybe he needed a backup pair for when these got wet. "Would tomorrow or the day after work? I can be flexible. I need new boots soon, but it's not a rush."

After taking his dishes to the sink, Dugan exited the kitchen more quickly than normal, with only a quick goodbye.

Sometimes I wish I could read that man's mind. Does he just want to be friends, or is he interested in something more?

Before she could leave the kitchen to clean up the formal dining room from the Rileys' breakfast, Jackson walked in carrying a few mostly empty serving dishes. "Good morning! I wanted to thank the lovely cook for such a delicious meal. You wouldn't be interested in coming to work for me when I get my house fixed up again, would you?"

Shaking her head, Gina replied, "No, thank you. I appreciate the offer, but I am thrilled to work right here for Nathan and Brianna. Dugan showed me what happened to your house. I'm sorry that happened to you, and I wish you the best of luck getting your house fixed."

Jackson shrugged and moved closer to Gina, not touching her but what she felt was inside her personal bubble. She didn't want to be rude and back up, but she was uncomfortable. "That's all right. Now that I've gotten used to the idea, I'm excited to get the chance to start over from scratch. The sky is the limit for what the new version of the house will look like. I'll have to give you a tour when it's finished."

Gina's eyes darted around, looking for an escape. "Thank you for the offer, but I'm sure I will see it if I ever need to bring a meal over for your father and you. Otherwise, this place keeps me way too busy for social calls."

Gina moved toward the sink and did dishes as an excuse to move away. He hadn't said or done anything inappropriate, but she couldn't help but be suspicious of such a confident, flirty man. Maxwell was rich, confident, and flirty too, and she didn't want to repeat the same mistakes. Was her refuge really as safe as she thought?

Chapter 26

Boot Shopping

G^{ina}

After getting approval for an afternoon off from Brianna, Gina sat in a mid-sized center console boat. They'd designed the boat with a double seat in the middle. Dugan sat in the captain's chair, smiling as he cruised along the ocean, and she sat nestled in the only other chair directly beside him. Oddly, she didn't mind the intimate setting. He only ever made her feel more comfortable and safe.

Getting approval from Brianna had been easier than she'd expected. At first, Brianna had reacted with shock when she realized that Gina had worked non-stop for the last few months without even taking a half-day off. She assured her she would talk with Nathan about giving her a raise and making sure she had regularly scheduled days off.

Then, with a mischievous grin that made her think Brianna was trying to do some matchmaking, she had brushed away her plans for preparing a cold lunch and being back in time for dinner. Brianna insisted they would be fine and not to worry about either lunch or dinner. In fact, she was welcome to take more time off as needed, as long as she let Brianna know in advance.

Gina felt the wind whipping through her hair as she looked up at Dugan beside her. He looked back down at her with his kind eyes that reminded her of the sea. Her heart beat faster, and for a moment, she thought he would lean down those last few inches and kiss her.

He stared at her wistfully as his lips parted, but to her utter disappointment, he turned back toward the wheel and used his mouth to talk instead. "So, there is a boot shop only a block from the beach that I thought we would stop in, and then I have to make a quick stop nearby." Dugan kept his head facing forward, but she caught him watching her intently from the corner of his eye. "Then, if you're hungry, I thought we could get something to eat. There's a food stand near the beach where we could pick up something and eat on the sand or a cafe we could stop in." Before she could respond, he hurriedly added, "Of course, if you don't want to, we can always just head back to the island. I just thought we might get hungry is all."

Gina's heart was still beating fast, and it took all of her control to slow it down. Boot shopping is about as romantic as heating up a Pop Tart is cooking. *He must not be interested, or he would have asked me on a date.* Boots. *I need to focus on the boot shopping. There sure isn't anything sensual about that.*

Keeping her voice calm, Gina said, "That sounds like a plan. I'm sure I will be hungry. What was it you needed to get after the boots? I could run and pick it up for you while you're trying on boots."

Frowning, Dugan shook his head. "Oh, you don't need to worry about that. It will take me just a few moments to get it. I know exactly what I need. Besides, I need my professional boot shopper to help me find the magic pair. Is there anything you would like to grab while we're in town?"

Shaking her head, Gina said, "No, I have everything I need. A quicker stop at the mainland sounds good to me."

***

The long ride to shore seemed to go quickly and pleasantly. She had to admit, it was refreshing to be out on the sea and away from the island. Although, once they got on shore, Gina couldn't help but constantly look over her shoulder. While they were walking to the shoe store, she spotted a man with short black hair that was about the same build as Maxwell. She froze and panicked until he turned, and the man's face assured her it wasn't him.

I need to calm down and stop being so paranoid. Focus on Dugan. Focus on boots. Forget about Maxwell.

Boot shopping turned out to be pretty straightforward and didn't take too long. She helped Dugan pick out a handful of options in his size. He dutifully tried them all on, but he ended up buying another copy of the same boots he wore. He checked out, and they walked out to the boardwalk.

Dugan pointed at a small food stand down by the beach. "Do you want to head down to decide on what you would like to eat? I just have to pick that thing up and I'll be right with you. Wait for me there. My treat for coming with me and helping me with the boots."

Gina looked at him suspiciously but replied, "Sure." He hurried off at a fast walk to a shop on the boardwalk three stores down from where she was. A part of her wanted to follow and see where he was going. She almost thought he was getting her a gift, except for the fact that he obviously wasn't interested in her as anything more than a friend. *Why is he being so cagey?*

Deciding to let him keep his little secrets, she went down to the food stand and looked over the menu. She was getting hungry and thought a nearby bench on the sand would be the perfect place to have their pleasant, low-key meal together. She walked over to the bench and sat down to make sure no one else stole it while she was waiting. Taking off her sandals, she buried her toes in the hot grains of sand.

Feeling glad that she had faced her fears about coming to the mainland, her eyes searched the boardwalk, looking for the large figure of Dugan returning to her. Instead, an icy fear pierced her chest as she saw *him*.

Maxwell's hair was a little longer than the last time she'd seen him, but he was unmistakable. He walked confidently down the boardwalk in a high-end dress shirt and suit pants, making sure that everyone around him knew he had money. The fresh hope and freedom that was building inside Gina shriveled up as she dropped from the bench down onto the sand.

Hunched over in front of the bench, she kept her face turned toward the sea, hoping Maxwell would pass by without seeing her. It felt like forever of being too afraid to move when she felt a tap on her shoulder. She started, and an embarrassing yelp escaped her mouth as she looked up at Dugan towering above her.

Bags in hand, Dugan's eyebrows creased in concern. "Gina! There you are. I was looking all over. You were hard to spot down there. Is everything all right?"

Gina couldn't look him in the eyes as she quietly responded, "I'm not feeling so great anymore. I think I got too much sun. Can we forget about food and just head back to Riley's Paradise Island?"

He held out a hand to help her up. "Sure. I can put the cover over the boat on our ride back to give you some shade, and I'll pick you up some water before we go to make sure you are well hydrated."

He didn't look her in the eye as he held a bag out toward her. "Here, maybe this will help. I picked up something for you too."

She glanced around, making sure the coast was clear before taking the bag. Without watching her open it, he immediately walked over to the nearby food stand and was paying for a water bottle. Dugan was so thoughtful and sweet. She really wished she hadn't ruined their outing.

Chapter 27

The Sketchy Sketch

Gina

Gina whistled to herself as she made her way down the jungle path leading to the secret garden. She swung the sketchbook and pencil set in her hand back and forth as she walked, feeling the joy of new beginnings swell in her chest. It was a beautiful day, and the garden seemed like just the place to start drawing again.

Despite her disastrous trip to the mainland, she was determined to focus on her fresh start and secretly hoped Dugan stayed a central part of it. With the Rileys back on their island and all the new employees coming and going, there was always a lot to do. While they no longer had the sole companionship they started with, Dugan seemed to make a point of talking to her and hanging around to lend her a hand whenever he could. Maybe there was still hope of something more between them.

She must have taken a wrong turn in this jungle that all looked the same because before she knew it, she came across a riddle sticking out of the ground. It read:

I can be broken, given, kept, and crushed, yet I always remain whole. What am I?

Gina looked about her and saw nothing out of the ordinary other than this odd little sign. She walked a circle around it and decided the storm took out the rest of whatever went with this. She would need to ask Dugan what it was for later.

Turning to go, Gina stopped as the sun reflected a flash of copper from within the thick jungle. Pushing aside some vines, she stepped off the path and pushed some brush aside until she found a large copper heart mostly turned green from the weather dangling from a tree. A small inchworm made its way across the heart, and when she reached out to touch it, the heart spun, revealing the other side. It read, "Brianna, my heart beats only for you. Love, Nathan."

Overcome by the sweetness of the message, Gina opened her sketchbook and drew the heart with the inchworm on top but changed the names on the message. What would it feel like to find a love note from Dugan? She traced over her drawing with her finger, but then quickly shut the notebook.

He didn't seem like the romantic sort, and if he viewed her as anything more than just a friend, he would have asked her out on a date instead of boot shopping. Maybe she wasn't his type, or maybe his job was too much of his focus. Regardless, he never stepped over the line of just being friendly into romantic territory.

With an enormous sigh, Gina backtracked, trying to find her way back to the main path so she could continue to the secret garden.

Instead of filling her notebook full of hearts and the name of her crush like a middle-schooler, she needed to draw something more sensible. She figured Bingo the llama was about as far from fanciful as she could get.

Looking around, Gina spotted a few trees that looked familiar. Were they familiar because she was on the right path now or because she'd spotted them while walking down the wrong path? Honestly, so many trees looked the same that she couldn't even be sure of that much.

A rustle of a bush near the edge of the path made her freeze as she waited to see what emerged. *Dugan said there were no predators on this island, so I shouldn't have to run, right?*

Suzie burst through, tail wagging rapidly. Gina knelt to pet the dog and set her notebook down on the ground beside her. "What a good girl you are. It's nice to see you, Suzie Q. Are you doing security rounds with Dugan?"

The dog gave a small yip, and a few minutes later, Dugan came around the bend of the path. Upon seeing Gina, a smile grew across his features and made his eyes light up. "Gina! How nice to run into you. Are you out taking a walk?"

Gina stood up. "I came to make some sketches out here, but I got turned around. I'm glad I ran into you two."

Dugan bent over and scooped up the notebook. "I'm glad you're using the notebook I got you. It's good to see you doing something you enjoy. Do you mind if I look?"

Snatching the notebook out of his hands, Gina held it close to her chest and wouldn't look him in the eye. "Um... I just started drawing and I haven't finished anything yet. Maybe later."

Holding up his hands, Dugan backed up a step and spoke in a lighthearted, teasing tone. "Don't worry. I won't look if you don't want me to. I'll let you keep your secrets."

Lamely, Gina halfheartedly tried to defend herself. "It's just llamas and stuff from the island."

"Sure, whatever you say. Do you want me to escort you to where you wanted to go?"

"If you wouldn't mind pointing me toward the secret garden, I would appreciate it. You don't have to come with me. I just want to draw some more llamas."

Dugan chuckled and walked down the path he'd come from. Gina followed. "I never knew that your passion for drawing focuses on an animal. Bingo must have really made an impression on you, that lucky guy. I'll walk with you. The secret gardens are part of my rounds today anyway."

***

Gina sat on a bench in the gardens, watching a butterfly flit from flower to flower. Dugan checked on the animals' food and water, collected eggs, and then told her he would see what fresh vegetables he could pick for her. He was now in the vegetable patch, filling up a bucket, obviously in no hurry to leave.

Taking her time, Gina sketched Bingo, a few of the funny fluffy chickens pecking about, and the stone wall with vines creeping over it, a beautiful purple flower accenting it. It felt great to use her creative skills. It felt like her stream of creativity had dried up and was finally drizzling again. She was feeling quite content and knew she would come back, but unfortunately, she needed to get back for mealtime.

She shut her notebook and made her way to the vegetable patch. She didn't want to interrupt whatever Dugan was busy working on but also didn't want to take off without saying something to him first. "Dugan, I just wanted to let you know that I need to head back so I can start making dinner and put the last few things together for Jenna's birthday party tomorrow."

Dugan held up an overflowing bucket. "Good, my bucket is full. Do you feel better after your drawing time? Not that I would dare ask to see again, but you certainly look more relaxed."

Rolling her eyes, Gina flipped her sketchbook open to the page with Bingo on it as Dugan made his way toward her. She had added her favorite character, Puss in Boots, riding on his back and brandishing a sword. His eyebrows shot up. "Gina, that's beautiful. I can't believe you captured such detail with only a pencil and even made the little fellow look like he has some attitude. It should never embarrass you to show off your art."

Gina flipped the page to the picture of the stone wall, keeping the rest of the pages firmly shut so Dugan didn't get an accidental peek of the copper heart with his name on it. He traced his finger over her drawing. "It's good to see you draw things other than llamas. Wow, look at your shading technique. It's so lifelike. This is stunning. Would you draw a few for me to frame and place around my cottage? I'll compensate you, of course."

Ducking her head, Gina shut her sketchbook. She would make him a drawing of his cottage overlooking the shoreline, and one of Suzie... in boots. "Yes, I'll make you some, but you don't have to pay me. I'm still working off your window I broke."

Dugan shook his head. "Gina, you never owe me anything."

Chapter 28

Jenna's Birthday Party

G ina

Gina stood at the back of the room and watched as all the Rileys loudly sang *Happy Birthday*.

Nathan pointed at the candles on the beautifully decorated three-layer cake Gina had made. "Make a wish and blow out your candles, birthday girl."

She'd had so much fun decorating and making a special dessert for the little girl. She'd used fondant to make miniature bird-of-paradise flowers to cover it and used three live flowers to pop out of the top. Jenna had audibly gasped in appreciation when she saw it and that alone made it all worthwhile.

Jenna scrunched up her face in concentration and then blew all her candles out in one breath. Everyone clapped and then talked amongst themselves. Gina approached the cake to cut it up and serve it, while she overhead Jenna say to her father, "I made a wish for a kitten instead of a baby brother or sister."

Nathan ran his hand through his hair and knelt down to be at eye level with his daughter. "Sweetheart, I know there have been a lot of changes in your life lately, but a baby brother or sister is going to be a great thing for us. The baby won't be able to do much when he or she is little, but there is no one on this earth that can be as good a big sister to him or her as you." Nathan bopped her gently on the nose and moved closer to speak conspiratorially. "So, I wasn't going to tell you this yet, but Dugan is talking about having Suzie have puppies again soon. Brianna and I are so impressed with how mature you are becoming that we asked him if you could have one. Dugan got so excited about the idea that he said you could have the very first pick of the litter!"

Gina was starting to place pieces of cake on plates when Jenna squealed, "Hooray! A puppy of my very own! BEST DAY EVER!" She started running around the room excitedly. Throwing herself at Debbie's legs, she looked up at her and quickly exclaimed, "I'm getting a puppy!"

Brianna moved closer. Her cute little stomach bump was getting very obvious now. "You told her, didn't you? I thought we were going to wait until Suzie had the next batch of pups."

Nathan ducked his head as he looked back at her. "I didn't think it could wait. She's scared about all the changes happening on the island and with our family, and I wanted to give her something she could look forward to and have some control over."

"I trust your judgment." Brianna picked up a piece of cake with a pretty flower and placed it in front of Jenna, then took a second piece for herself. Gina kept cutting and serving, then she took the remaining cake back into the kitchen. Brianna had suggested she offer it to the staff if they wanted it.

Dugan walked into the room and snagged a piece of cake for himself before taking a seat at the kitchen table. He took a large bite. "You outdid yourself with this cake. It's delicious! I also peeked in and saw the decorations you did in that room before the party started. You have a genuine gift."

Her cheeks flushed as she took a piece of cake and sat down beside Dugan. "I'm glad you like it. I enjoyed making the cake and decorating, but honestly, I'm getting pretty worn out. It's been a lot doing all the cooking for so many people, and I have been trying to do some light house cleaning to help Brianna keep up with things until a full-time housekeeper comes. She's just exhausted all the time and really only seems to have the energy to care for Jenna and not much else right now."

Dugan finished his cake before Gina even took her second bite. "Actually, we have a lead in that direction. I talked with Nathan this morning about how Tim's wife is currently part of a hotel cleaning crew. Tim has a wife and a seven-year-old little boy living on the mainland that he hasn't gotten to see a lot over the last few months. Nathan's considering hiring Tim to be our permanent maintenance employee and his wife to be a part-time housekeeper. They would homeschool on the island like Brianna is doing with Jenna, and it would give the little girl a peer to play with. Hopefully, it will all work out."

Gina nodded her head. "That will be nice for Jenna to have a play-mate." She pushed her finished plate away and crossed her arms on the table in front of her. She looked up at him with one eyebrow raised. "So, you're having puppies again?"

Dugan jerked his head backward in surprise. "How did you hear about that already? Nathan and I just talked about it for the first time today. I told him about what a success Pongo has been, and I was hoping for one more pup that would be suitable to train and pair up with my other security employee, Buck. Nathan asked if Jenna could have a puppy for herself, and I heartily agreed. I've noticed Jenna's growing up and wanting more and more independence. Besides being a cute new best friend, I could train the dog to be her personal security dog as well."

Laughing to herself, Gina patted him on the shoulder as she stood up. "You really live and breathe security, don't you?"

Dugan furrowed his brow and gave a curt nod. "I have always taken my job seriously, but after that man kidnapped Brianna right under my nose on this island I am supposed to protect, I feel like I can't ever let my guard down. I can't let someone I'm supposed to protect get hurt."

Laying her hand back on his shoulder, she tried to comfort him. "You do an amazing job, and I've never felt safer anywhere else in my life, but you know you can't always keep everyone safe. Sometimes accidents happen or people do things that are outside of your control."

Dugan set his lips stubbornly as he looked up at her. "I would lay down my life to protect anyone on this island." She felt like he was talking specifically to her, and she believed him.

The door crashed open as Jackson carried some dishes into the kitchen. Gina jumped away from Dugan and hurried over to take them. As he handed them over, he gave her a large, charming smile and said, "I just wanted to help the world's most beautiful chef."

Gina stiffened at his flattery, but Jackson didn't seem to notice as he continued, "Thank you for that delicious birthday meal for Jenna. My niece had a wonderful time, and it's all thanks to you."

She kept her words concise as she replied, "I'm glad she enjoyed it." Then she moved out to the formal dining room to clean up after the party. As she was leaving, she heard Dugan's chair make a loud screech as he got up. He approached Jackson, and she thought she heard Dugan say something to the effect of her being one of those women who appreciates a bit of space.

She was so caught up in her thoughts that she didn't even notice Debbie re-enter the room. Gina jumped as she spoke. "Gina, this party was wonderful. You have way surpassed my skills as the Rileys' cook. Thank you for making the day so special for Jenna. It meant a lot to her."

Gina smiled. Debbie seemed friendly, and Jenna adored her, but the woman had only arrived yesterday, and she was still trying to get a feel for her. "That's very kind. Thank you."

Debbie took a deep breath and spoke faster. "So, I feel kind of awkward asking this because, until recently, I was the help, but Walter and I were talking and we both feel you would be the perfect person to plan a little wedding for us in three weeks, right here on the island. It would be a minor affair, with only a dozen more people than were here at this party and, of course, if you are interested, there would be extra financial compensation as well. What do you think?"

Gina raised her eyebrows and stared at Debbie, speechless. She already felt overwhelmed by the amount of work she had to do. On the other hand, this was an enormous honor to be asked, and she didn't want to let the Rileys down. Her staying in this refuge depended on them.

Gathering her composure, Gina calmly replied, "Sure. What colors were you thinking?"

Chapter 29

Teeny Tiny Bows

Gina

Gina looked out over the supplies for fifty favors she had spread across the kitchen table and countertops. She had bought small green succulents that she was going to transplant into miniature pots. The pots were going to be wrapped in burlap with a small, light pink bow around it. She had printed tiny flags saying "Debbie & Walter, Let Love Grow" to place inside each pot.

She was sure they would look adorable when she finished them, but they were going to be so much work to finish putting together. She had about a week until the wedding, and she was desperately trying to get all the decorations crossed off her list so she could focus on the cake and food during the last days leading up to the reception.

Gina felt like she could cry. It was past ten o'clock already, and all she had completed toward preparing for the wedding was organizing her supplies for the favors. Keeping up with everything around her was utterly exhausting. After a long day of trying to cook and clean up after the six Rileys living in Nathan's compound and the seven employees that had been coming and going, depending on her for meals between shifts, she was having a hard time squeezing in time for wedding planning.

The new housekeeper, Martha, wasn't starting until after the wedding, and the ceremony was becoming a much bigger production than the dozen people she was originally thinking when Debbie asked her to plan it. She was all on her own, and she had nothing left to give. Burying her face in her hands, Gina sat there, immobilized. She didn't think she could do it.

Dugan walked into the kitchen, Suzie on his heels. Upon entering the room, he paused and seemed to take in the mess of supplies covering every flat surface. Tentatively, he asked, "What are you still doing here, Gina? Shouldn't you be back in your apartment sketching llamas in boots by now?" He gestured toward the supplies. "What is all of this for?"

Between sniffles, she looked up from her hands. "I'm in way over my head with this wedding. I just have too much going on trying to take care of all the meals and cleaning. When Debbie asked me to plan the wedding, I felt honored. She said it would be just a few more guests than the Rileys, and I thought that meant less than a dozen. I know fifty people is typically a smaller wedding, but it's a lot for me. I've never cooked for that large of a group before, and I'm so tired and overwhelmed that I can't even bring myself to start on these favors."

Dugan walked over to the stove and put a kettle on to warm up. He grabbed two mugs, two chamomile tea bags, a sugar bowl, and a few leftover chocolate chip cookies from the fridge. He placed everything down in front of Gina and sat in the chair next to her. "What can I do to help?"

Gina smiled up at him gratefully as she added a scoop of sugar to her tea, mixing it gently with a spoon. "Nothing, really. I just need to suck it up and get back to work, I guess. Thanks for listening to me whine. I already feel like I can start on this project… after I finish my tea and cookies with you."

Dugan dipped a chocolate chip cookie into his tea and ate half of it in one bite. "I'm serious. Show me how to put together these little plant things, and I'll help you. You can be the boss, and I will be your faithful servant."

Rolling her eyes at him playfully, she put her hand over his and said, "Thank you. I really appreciate the offer, but I have to warn you that even with the two of us, we will probably still be here for hours."

He took a hand and moved a stray hair away from her eyes. "If it keeps you from having to spend all night long doing this, then it's a few hours well spent. Where do we start?"

Gina looked over her supplies, figuring out the best way to break up the tasks. "I'll start putting the burlap covers on the pots. If you would plant all the little succulents into them, does that sound good?"

After they finished their tea and cookies, they got to work, but it swiftly became apparent that the burlap part took a lot longer than planting. Dugan's large hands engulfed one of the mini pots as he held it up and examined it. "Here, show me how you do the burlap and tie that tiny bow."

Gina lifted a single eyebrow and cocked her head. "You want to learn how to tie little bows?"

Dugan nodded, so she showed him how she tightly wrapped the pot in burlap while securing the insides with a glue gun. Dugan caught on to that step pretty quickly but struggled with forming the tight, delicate bow.

Taking his large hands into her own, she showed him how she tied it using only the tips of her fingers. He did one on his own and looked up to her with a smile of triumph. It immediately died on his lips, and she became conscious of just how close she was to him.

As his hand tightened around her own, she felt his breath quicken. A thrill of exhilaration rushed through her body, along with the need to be held, kissed, and cherished. She froze, both wanting to feel the brush of his lips on hers and afraid of where it would lead. *I need to stop reading into these intimate moments with him. They lead nowhere and are obviously all in my head.*

While his hand still covered Gina's, Dugan's voice came out thicker and deeper than normal. He quietly asked her, "Gina, would you like to go on a picnic with me?"

Chapter 30

Otter Cove Picnic

G*ina*

They sat on a blanket on the beach of the island's cove watching an otter and her pup romp and play in the water. It was the most adorable thing Gina had ever seen. Her bare toes wiggled in the sand as she sat on a picnic blanket. She felt so much better after taking a break from her busy day. She needed to make that a priority so she didn't get burned out.

Dugan unpacked a basket that sat beside him. He brought out simple sandwiches, fresh fruit, and chocolates. It wasn't the fanciest feast she had eaten, but in a way, that made it even more special. He wouldn't let her into the kitchen as he prepared their picnic lunch, telling her he didn't want to ruin the surprise. She was delighted that he was making the effort to do all this for her. That he thought she was worth the effort.

Maxwell would have demanded she pack a big fancy multi-course picnic and then complained because she didn't guess what he was in the mood for. She vowed to stop comparing the two. On the surface, Maxwell looked like the full package. Rich, handsome, and well-connected. From the surface, no one would understand why she would cringe at the thought of being with Maxwell and crave to be with a man like Dugan.

She had learned the hard way that appearances weren't what was important. There really wasn't anything to compare between the two when Dugan won in every category that mattered. Gina knew she needed to stop focusing on the past and move forward. She was on her first date with a man who appreciated her for her, and she didn't want to spend it thinking about the regrets of her past. Gina would not let the doubts and fears Maxwell planted in her mind rule her life. Pushing him out of her mind felt like she was taking an immense weight off her shoulders. She was closing one chapter of her life as she embraced the new one.

Before she could think about it and convince herself not to, Gina leaned back onto Dugan's large, brawny chest. She heard his heart beating loudly and steadily, and he slowly and cautiously brought one of his arms around to hold her closer to him. She nestled deeper into Dugan's embrace, and he tightened his arm around her. He felt so comforting and safe, like she was a puzzle piece created to nestle perfectly under his chin.

The otter's mother lay out on her back and floated around while the kit climbed up onto his mother's stomach, nestled under her chin, and fell soundly asleep. They quietly watched the otters float until they heard Pongo bark from a distance. The disturbed otters slipped under the water and swam off out of sight.

Dugan shifted and used his free hand to pull his phone out of his pocket to look at it. Gina moved out of his embrace to look at him face to face. While leaning on one arm, she glanced down at his phone and then up at him. "Everything all right? You can go if you need to."

Dugan furrowed his brow. "I didn't get a message, so whatever Pongo found must be something Susan can handle on her own. Probably another squirrel or something. That pup is really smart, but he still has a way to go to complete his training."

Dugan looked up from his phone and into her eyes. He reached out and took her hand into his own, and she thought she saw the same yearning that she felt. "I shouldn't have checked my phone. I'm sorry, it's a habit. Right now, I don't care what else is going on. Gina, I don't want to be anywhere else but here with you."

He dropped her hand, lifted a plastic-wrapped sandwich, and held it out to her. "Would you like something to eat?" He looked at the sandwich and then moved to put it back down. "I'm sorry, it's not anything fancy. I'm not great in the kitchen like you are. We could try going to the mainland again, and I could take you out to a real nice restaurant."

Slightly too loudly, Gina said, "No!" as she grabbed the sandwich from him. She settled back down and looked up at him through her eyelashes. "This is perfect. I don't need big fancy dinners on the mainland. I think this simple picnic on the beach, just the two of us, is the most romantic thing we could do."

Gina leaned over and gave Dugan a quick kiss on the cheek before unwrapping her sandwich. She was pleased to see him raise his hand and place it on his cheek where her lips had touched moments before.

"Thank you for putting this together. There is nowhere else I would rather be either."

Dugan took a bite of his own sandwich. "So, how is the wedding planning going? I really appreciate you taking some time to have lunch with me when I know you're so busy. If you want, I can help tie some more bows again this evening. I think I was finally getting the hang of it when we finished the favors last night."

Smiling up at him, Gina thought about how much more refreshed she felt since the night before. Yes, she was making good progress with the wedding plans, but she also thought the new rush of feelings for Dugan probably had something to do with it. After he had asked her on a date, it seemed like the entire world became more vibrant. Like she could tackle anything as long as Dugan was by her side.

"I appreciate the excuse for a break. You were right. I was working myself to exhaustion and needed a rest, but even though there are only a few days left until the wedding, I feel like I'm in a good place now. I have all the decorations ready, and this morning I worked on a lot of the food that could be prepared ahead of time. Right now, the refrigerator and freezer are full and ready for the wedding day. The day of the wedding will still be pretty busy setting everything up and making all the fresh food, but I think it will turn out nicely. I hope Debbie and Walter like it."

Raising an eyebrow at Dugan, she asked sweetly, "Would you mind organizing a few guys to help set up tables, tents, and chairs near the waterfall? That's where the ceremony and reception are going to take place. We're also going to need some people stationed at the docks the day of the wedding to escort guests."

Grabbing a fresh strawberry, Dugan offered her the container. "I will have a meeting with all the island personnel this afternoon and create a job duty chart. Honestly, we should have done this sooner. You don't have to do everything yourself. We will all pull together to make this happen. Tell us what you want and we'll set everything up. All you need to worry about is the food."

She felt a warm feeling inside at the thought of her friends all coming together to help her. She really wasn't on her own anymore.

Dugan pulled out the pudding cup and a spoon and held them out to her. "Pudding cup?"

Chapter 31

The Mysterious Box

G ina

Sitting on the loveseat in her cozy apartment, Gina was taking a few minutes to herself after preparing and cleaning up after lunch. She held the decorative metal box that she'd found on the beach with Dugan and turned it around in her hands, examining every angle.

There had to be a trick to opening it, and she was determined not to ask for help. She wanted Dugan to think of her as clever enough to figure it out herself. Dugan volunteered to tell her where it went on the island after she figured out its trick, and she couldn't wait to see how the complete puzzle fit together.

She traced some of the geometric shapes that covered the outside, but none of them budged, no matter how she tried to push on them. While pulling on one shape, she accidentally pushed the top third of the box. It twisted one full rotation before it wouldn't budge anymore. One of the geometric shapes that looked like a diamond could now swivel outwards, and another part of the box was able to twist.

Totally focused, Gina lost track of time as she twisted and extended parts of the box until it left her with a T shape. She held it up and tried to move the pieces more, but the only direction they would go was back the way they'd come from. Then she realized the shapes sticking out of the shaft of the T were all different lengths, just like a key. The box unraveled to open something, but what?

Looking at the clock, Gina realized her break was over. She needed plenty of time to make a large enough meal to feed everyone on the island, and sweet little Jenna always squealed with delight when she had the time to make dessert too. After packing up her things, she placed the key into the small backpack she carried around the island with her. She hummed with excitement. She couldn't wait to show Dugan after dinner that she had finally figured it out.

***

Gina finished packing up the last of the lobster rolls after dinner when Dugan walked over carrying a few dishes to the sink for her. He was always so helpful. "Hey, Dugan. Do you mind sticking around for a few minutes after I finish cleaning up? I want to show you something."

Giving her a broad smile, Dugan looked like he couldn't be happier about the request. "I feel like a cat with a box. What do you want to show me?" He turned on the hot water and washed some of the large dishes that didn't fit into the dishwasher.

Gina stepped over Suzie, who lay on the floor, in order to sit her backpack on the counter. "I need a little break from all the wedding preparations. Are you ready for a little adventure tonight?"

"Always. Show me what you've got."

Unzipping her backpack, she took out the large metal key and set it on the countertop before picking up a towel and hand-drying the dishes Dugan washed. She watched Dugan intently, curious to catch his reaction. She caught a flicker of a smile across his face.

Dugan cocked his head. "You figured it out! With so much going on, I forgot all about it. I'm impressed you figured it out without needing any help. That's a hard one. After we finish these last few dishes and I grab some flashlights, we can head toward the docks. The puzzle that goes to isn't too far from there."

"Are we going to be out that long?"

"You'll see."

***

Suzie sniffed the jungle pathway and ventured into the brush in front of Dugan and Gina. Monkeys hooted in the trees around her, making her think of Chee Chee. He was cute while Dugan was watching over him, but the little fellow seemed happiest as Brianna's constant companion.

Dugan stopped short, and Gina ran into him. He caught her by the shoulders and pointed to the branch of a tree they'd passed. Gina stared, still not seeing anything, until one eye of a chameleon moved slightly. Only her beast master would have been able to spot that guy. He whispered, "Come on. It's not much farther."

They walked until they came to what looked like a large rock covered in branches, leaves, and moss. Dugan cleared it away and then started moving the debris out of the way beside the rock too. "Here we are."

Gina looked down to see the rock was manmade. At the top was an empty square socket that seemed to be about the size of the ornamental box Gina found, and below it was a hole. Dugan pointed toward the square shape. "That box usually fits pretty snugly on here, but a branch must have knocked it loose. Then either a strong wind or a curious monkey must have carried it the rest of the way to the shoreline where you found it. I'm honestly pretty shocked that we didn't lose it for good, and this would have been just another puzzle that I would have had to dissemble or fix after the hurricane."

Taking the key out of her backpack, Gina held it up. "Can I put the key in the hole?"

Dugan nodded his head. "Sure, go ahead. You already figured out the hard part."

After placing the key in the hole, Gina turned it and heard a satisfying click. The rock moved to the left, leaving an opening that led to the cave system. Everything was pitch black, unlike the areas she'd seen before. "I'm glad you brought the flashlights now. What about Suzie?"

Dugan handed Gina one of the lights. "Since the cave system leads to Nathan's control room, he wanted all entrances secured. This one is far out of the way, so we never use it, but at least we know someone can't easily sneak in and mess with the security system. We don't need to worry about Suzie. She will wait here for us. Are you ready for a little spelunking?"

Gina nodded. "After you."

Chapter 32

Crystal Caves

D ugan

Dugan watched Gina walk beside him out of the corner of his eye, his palms sweating despite the cool cave around them. His mind wouldn't stray from the thought of kissing this woman. Every waking moment focused on her, and he didn't think he could go on without tasting her lips.

She was so beautiful, smart, hardworking, and kind. He had nothing to offer her but himself, but so far, she seemed receptive to his quiet, subtle advances. He was ready to be bold and declare his feelings, but he was so very nervous. His dog would love him every day, no matter what, but who knew how a woman's mind worked? Dugan braced himself for rejection, but even if there was only an infinitesimal chance he could win over a woman like Gina, he had to try.

The cave came to a Y, and Dugan led her to the right. Gina followed close behind. "How do you know which way to go? Please tell me you aren't just guessing and we're not about to spend the next week down here eating rats in the pitch dark."

Dugan chuckled. "There aren't any rats down this deep because they don't have any food sources down here, but you don't have to worry. When I first worked for Nathan, I mapped these tunnels to make sure that all entrances were secured and then memorized them."

"Wow, you really take your job seriously, don't you?"

Gina tripped over a rock and grabbed Dugan's arm to catch her balance. He was pleased when she didn't take that hand away. "I sure do. It's my responsibility to keep this island safe, and I will do everything in my power to make sure that happens. Against my personal wishes for solitude, I even hired Susan and Buck to help with security when it became apparent that it was too large a job for one man. What matters is the safety of this island's inhabitants."

Gina asked in a quiet voice, "Are you sad Nathan hired these employees?"

Dugan placed his right hand over the top of Gina's, which was holding onto his left arm. "Like a polar bear in a desert, I would happily live in the middle of a big city if it meant I got to meet you." He wondered if she realized just how hard it would be for him to live around that many people and how much he was willing to give up for her.

After a few more turns and bends, Dugan stopped in front of a narrow hole not much bigger than himself. He turned to Gina. "I want you to go into the next cavern first."

"Am I about to be eaten by a dragon or cave bear or something?"

Dugan squeezed her hand on his arm. "Don't worry, you can trust me. I'll be right behind you so we can get eaten together."

Gina eyed him for a few minutes, as if reassuring herself that he was kidding. Then she took a deep breath before letting go of him, bending over, and walking through the hole. He heard her gasp from the next room, so he hurried through the hole, not to see the next room's majesty but to see Gina's face and bask in her awe.

Giant crystal prisms stretched from the cave ceiling to the ground all around them. The light from their flashlights glittered as it bounced around the room and caught off some of the clear stalactites hanging from the ceiling. The effect was magical as Gina moved her flashlight around rapidly, trying to take in the gorgeous giant crystals around them.

Dugan moved so that his back was to the crystals. He had seen them all before, and he had a clear view of Gina. "So, what do you think? Worth solving that puzzle?"

Gina's jaw hung open as her wide eyes continued to take in her dazzling surroundings. "I can't believe this. I didn't think this island could get more amazing, but you keep surprising me."

Dugan moved forward and put one arm around Gina as he pointed to a clear crystal prism to their left. "Look at this. If I point my flashlight at just the right angle..."

"You made a rainbow come out the other side! That's amazing! Thank you so much for showing me this. I've never seen anything like it before in my life."

Still cradling her in one of his arms, Dugan turned his head down toward Gina, watching her look around in awe. He knew the natural beauty around him would never again satiate his eyes as he gazed upon her heart-shaped face. Uncaring about the surrounding crystals, Dugan knew he would never see anything more beautiful in his whole life than her. "Gina, may I kiss you?"

Impossibly, Gina's eyes grew even wider as they moved from the crystals to focus on his eyes. Instead of answering, she reached up and threw her arms around his neck, pulling him down until his lips reached hers. He wrapped his arms around her small waist, dropping his flashlight, and lights and colors bounced around the room as he kissed her like he had wanted to since first meeting her.

He tried to be slow and gentle, but Gina's eager kisses started a fire burning within him that he couldn't douse. He matched her passionate pace, and his joy grew knowing that she truly wanted him. Gina's lips partially parted, and Dugan ran his tongue against them, causing her to let out a soft moan.

Gina took control of him, pressing her mouth and slight body firmly against his own. He covered her with his lips, holding onto her tightly lest he lose control of himself and the craving he felt for her. *I love this woman. I want her to be mine. Forever.*

She broke away from his kiss, and he moved his head away, trying not to show his disappointment. He enjoyed the feel of her but didn't want to push things too fast. Before he got far, Gina planted soft little pecks on his neck below his ear. He gasped out, "Oh, Gina," before engulfing her in more ardent kisses.

Chapter 33

The Big Day

Gina

Everything was going perfectly. They decorated the tables with white linen tablecloths and large vases filled with various jungle flowers and the succulent favors Dugan helped her put together. Pots of additional flowers lined the entire clearing, and fairy lights woven through the trees made the clearing near the waterfall look magical.

Dugan had the security personnel escorting guests in small groups from their boats through the jungle. The food looked as beautiful as she hoped it tasted, and it was all packaged protectively for the construction crew to deliver to the tables set up near the waterfall. Tim's wife, Martha, who was going to be their new housekeeper, was even able to come out to the island a bit early to help her set up and serve the food. Everyone was really coming together, just like a family.

Ticking off her fingers, Gina tried to make sure she wasn't missing anything. The pastor arrived, and the orchestra quartet was currently setting up for the ceremony. Both the bride and groom were getting ready in different parts of Nathan's compound, where she had provided them with snacks and refreshments before the ceremony. Jenna was as full of energy as ever, and Gina periodically caught sight of her escaping in her flower girl dress to snag a cheese stick or pilfer a cookie from the kitchen.

Picking up a tall, hefty box, Gina was carrying the wedding cake to the reception herself. After the many hours she'd spent on it, she didn't trust anyone else to do this job. It needed to be kept level while she carried it, but luckily, she had planned for having to transport it. Instead of making one humongous cake and trying to transport it through the jungle, she and Debbie had decided to do one small decorative cake for pictures and cutting, but the cake for the guests would come from a similarly decorated sheet cake.

She heard the wedding party laughing and joking happily as they left Nathan's compound to start the ceremony. It was time to set up the food. Carefully, she picked up the cake box and started on her way out of the compound. *I wonder what Dugan is up to right now. I know he was checking in guests at the dock to make sure they allowed only invited guests ashore. Maybe I will catch sight of him doing perimeter checks around the wedding reception.*

She pictured his enormous form stealthily sneaking through the jungle's thick foliage, constantly surveying the guests and making sure no suspicious hooligans were up to no good. He took his job seriously, and she felt safe knowing he was on the lookout.

Moving slowly down the path, Gina took extra care with every root and stray branch. All she had to do was get the cake there in one piece. It wasn't hard, and she must have walked these trails hundreds of times at this point.

Humming along to herself, Gina thought about her date with Dugan. She was a bit surprised at how slowly he was taking things, but that was perfectly fine with her. She wanted to know everything about him, both his good days and his bad ones, before getting serious.

The thought of making a commitment surprised her. Only a few months ago, she'd convinced herself that she would never be in a relationship again. Now she found herself not only wanting to be with Dugan, but she could imagine a future with him too.

She could move into his cozy little cottage with him, and they could both look after Riley's Paradise Island together. She pictured them wrinkled and gray, standing arm in arm, looking out over the ocean. One of Suzie's descendants would lie at their feet as they watched the sunset from the comforts of the island that had become their home.

Gina got to the drawbridge that allowed people to cross the roaring stream below. She frowned to herself. The bridge was up. When talking with Dugan, they'd decided to set the bridge mechanisms to keep it down during the whole ceremony and reception. That way, guests could come and go as they pleased without having to solve a puzzle first.

Shrugging, Gina figured she would just tell him when she got over there. She didn't know what had gone wrong, but this was a pretty minor inconvenience she could easily fix. As carefully as possible, Gina laid the cake box on the ground. She had to act quickly so an ant or a monkey didn't find a way inside and decide to help themselves to her perfectly crafted confection.

It looked like someone had taken the hydraulic pump out of the water. With a sigh, she threw it back in, trying not to get herself wet. Within a few moments, the drawbridge started to lower.

As Gina made her way into the clearing, she could hear the pastor talking into the microphone about marriage and commitment and growing together with love. There weren't more than fifty people in attendance, mostly family and friends, but they wanted to make sure they could hear him over the background noise of the falls.

So far, it sounded like things were going exactly as planned. She knew they had set the chairs up so that everyone would be looking at the happy couple near the waterfall. Her goal was to slip in the back and quietly get all the food set up, so when they finished the ceremony, everyone would turn around and the food would have appeared like magic.

As she walked up, she gasped quietly at how beautifully everything had turned out. It was a dream wedding. Oddly, she wished she could have something similar someday, but on a smaller scale. Even if it was just her and Dugan, it would be perfect. *Getting ahead of myself, aren't I? It must be all the wedding fever in the air.*

She spotted her helper for the day, Martha. They made eye contact, and Gina gave her a bright, welcoming smile. She didn't dare talk because interrupting the wedding was the last thing she wanted. Martha gave a quick smile back but was already busy setting up chafing dishes to keep the food warm. Martha walked off to finish setting up the cookie table, and Gina followed, ready to lay down her precious load.

Out of the corner of her eye, she noticed a tall man with black hair turn around in the back row of the chairs set up to watch the ceremony. She turned to confirm what she feared, and her heart plummeted as a rush of shock and dread made it hard to breathe. The cake fell from her hands with a quiet thud, and icing splattered all around her feet. Standing a few yards in front of her, wearing a fine suit and a smirk, was Maxwell, and he was staring right at her.

Chapter 34

The Wedding Crasher

G^{ina}

No one turned when the cake fell. There must have been too much noise between the pastor talking and the background of the waterfall. Even Martha, who was only a few yards away arranging cookies, didn't turn around. Maxwell slipped out of his seat and kept his head held high as he smoothly walked toward her.

He smiled at her in his normally charming way. As charming as a snake ready to strike. His silky-smooth voice spoke quietly so only her ears would hear. "I found you. Walk with me so we can talk without interrupting this beautiful wedding." Panicking and looking around for Dugan, Gina didn't see any escape that didn't involve yelling and ruining the ceremony.

Gina whispered back, "I will walk with you to talk as long as you understand I am not leaving here with you."

Mouth slightly ajar, he blinked rapidly, but in the end, he quickly nodded his head. Cake already ruined, Gina left it lying where it fell. She destroyed it, just like the new life she'd built for herself was about to crumble to pieces. She felt sick to her stomach as she turned and walked back down the jungle path, Maxwell close on her heels.

They walked a few yards away when Gina stopped. While she didn't want to disrupt the wedding, she felt it safest to stay within yelling distance, just in case. Trying to keep her voice under control, Gina shook slightly as she asked him, "How did you find me?"

Maxwell reached out his hands toward hers, but Gina crossed her arms and took a step back. Maxwell dropped his arms but still looked imploringly into Gina's eyes. "I think it was fate. I saw you leaving at the beach a few weeks ago. You were gone before I could catch up to you, but I saw the store you came out of. A shoe store. I searched the boardwalk and couldn't find you, but that's when I knew you were somewhere nearby." He took a deep breath and gave her one of his charming half-smiles. "Regina, if you wanted me to pay more atten-tion to you, you could have just said so. You wanted to be pursued, so I went on the hunt."

A shiver ran down Gina's spine as she heard her full name come out of his mouth. He had made her hate that name.

Maxwell looked around him into the trees surrounding them. He spoke more swiftly than before. "Listen, you need to come home with me right now. You're in danger here, and I can't keep you safe in the middle of a jungle."

Mustering all the courage she had gained the last few months, Gina plainly and succinctly replied, forcing herself to look him in the eye so that he understood she wasn't the timid little girl he once bossed around. "Maxwell, I didn't leave because I wanted to be pursued. I left because I felt I had to escape a relationship with you. Yes, things started great, but then you got so overprotective and controlling. Every time I tried to express my unhappiness, you always manipulated my words so I felt like the bad guy for not letting you protect me. Having your men follow me everywhere made me feel unsafe, even going to the grocery store. I needed to get free of you."

He put his hand on her elbow and tried to guide her farther down the path. Gina resisted and didn't budge. She wished with all her might that Dugan would come walking around the corner. "I'm not going anywhere with you. I have a life here now, and we are done."

Maxwell ducked his head and looked at her through his lashes. "Regina, I love you. I just want to keep you safe like any good boyfriend would. I'm sorry that you felt so stifled. Can we go somewhere private to talk? I wasn't trying to be controlling. Please give me a chance to explain everything."

Gina thought about her options. She really didn't want to interrupt everyone at the wedding. She could yell for help, but what would she say? That she ruined the wedding because her ex-boyfriend was talking to her? He had a way with people where he would laugh and say that she was being overly dramatic, and she would come out of the situation looking like she was exaggerating.

He wouldn't stop. He would just keep on pursuing her and trying to manipulate her until she went with him. A plan was forming in her mind. She didn't want to abandon Martha, but the woman seemed to have everything under control. It went against every grain of her being to leave the wedding she worked so hard to prepare, but she could think of no other way to keep herself safe and not ruin the wedding.

If she went back to her apartment and locked herself in, maybe she could wait out this wedding and Maxwell's welcome. Speaking of welcome, how in the world did he get past security? Dugan himself would have checked Maxwell in as he did everyone attending this event. She couldn't exactly picture Maxwell sneaking onto the island and still looking so pristine in his expensive suit.

Choosing her words very cautiously, Gina gulped. "All right, I will go with you. We will talk back at my apartment, and you can explain how you making me feel like a prisoner in our home was just a misunderstanding."

They walked down the path, and Maxwell relaxed but didn't let his hand off of her elbow. Gina's mood darkened, but his genial voice returned. "Now, now. No need to get snippy. I know the Regina I know and love is still in there somewhere. It's probably a good idea to head back to your apartment so you can have a few minutes to grab your things before we get on the boat I rented. I want to leave before the wedding is over so we don't have to answer awkward questions."

Unable to stop her voice from quivering, she said, "I'm willing to listen, but I already told you I'm not leaving with you. How did you get here, anyway? There was a very exclusive invitation sent out for this wedding, and I know for a fact that security checked every person who came today."

He gave her a large grin as they neared her apartment. "After I couldn't find you at the beach, I went back to the boot store and asked them questions. They didn't know you, but they knew the employee you were with. A regular patron from Riley's Paradise Island."

He leaned down and kissed the top of her head. A shiver of dread ran through her body. "It was just like my little minx to play hide-and-seek right under my nose. My father was once friends with Walter Riley. It's amazing what a few phone calls can do when you know people."

Opening the front door, Gina turned and tried to sound casual as she said, "You don't need to come up with me. It will just take me a minute to run up and grab us some refreshing drinks and then we can sit in the nice common building while we chat. It will keep you from having to do the stairs, and it's a lot cooler there. I know it's a hot day out here today."

Squeezing her hand in a manner that would reassure her if it was coming from anyone else, he walked in the door and up the stairs with her. "Don't worry, I'll be with you to the end. I've been thinking a lot about it, and I think I know why you ran away. You were lonely, and I should have seen it sooner. I was only trying to keep you safe, but I didn't consider how you were feeling."

She stopped on the landing in front of her apartment door, stalling for time. Her plan wasn't working. She wished she could go back in time and tell Martha where she was going or refuse to leave the wedding, even if she had to make a disturbance.

He turned her to look at him. "When we get home, I will be more sensitive to your needs. We can start working on getting you a baby to take care of right away, so you will never be lonely again." He gave her a suggestive wink. "It will be fun."

Gina glared at Maxwell. She had to figure out a way to get away from this man before things got ugly. She wracked her brain while she kept him talking. "I wasn't lonely. You trapped me. The only one I needed protection from was you."

Aha, a trap! This island is full of them.

Maxwell's features grew still and serious. "I'm sorry I didn't tell you the truth before this, but I really was trying to keep you safe. Whatever you decide to do in the future is up to you, but right now, we have to get out of here before Jerry's men arrive."

Chapter 35

Finding Gina

D^{ugan}
Finishing up a security circuit around the compound, Dugan walked up to the wedding ceremony in time to see Walter Riley say, "I do." The old man looked like he was even smiling. Dugan never thought he would see the day when that happened. The crowd headed toward the reception tents. Looking around at the decorations, Dugan stared around in awe. Gina really outdid herself.

Little Jenna scampered by in her flower girl dress, scattering even more petals as her grandparents walked down the aisle after her. Brianna walked soon after with a hand over her growing belly and Chee Chee sitting contently on her shoulder.

Always thinking of Gina, Dugan's eyes scanned the crowd of people heading back to the reception tents for her familiar form. He saw Martha, Nathan's new housekeeper, scrambling to fill drinks and finishing setting up food all by herself. Where was Gina? This was her time to show off what a flawless wedding she had pulled off. Her beautiful smiling face should be here.

Dugan kept Suzie close to his heels as he made his way over to Martha. "Thanks for helping with the wedding today. You have been a lot of help. Do you know where I can find Gina? Is she feeling all right?"

Martha looked up at Dugan, wide-eyed and frazzled, with a few stray hairs going every which way. A bit curtly, she responded, "I don't know where she went. She was here one moment and gone the next. I came to help her out, and she left me to serve it all myself!"

Frowning, Dugan looked around the clearing again. "That's not like Gina at all. She is always the first and the last one working. Something isn't right. Susan made a trip to Nathan's compound. When she gets back, I'll have her monitor things here so I can go find out where Gina went."

The island was still full of traps and riddles that Gina didn't know about. Was she accidentally trapped somewhere? Dugan looked down to notice that Suzie had wandered away from his legs. He followed her to find the beautiful wedding cake that Gina spent hours working on splattered along the back of one of the tables.

His stomach twisted. He knew Gina had planned on carrying the cake herself. Was it possible she ran off after she dropped the cake, too upset to continue with the wedding, or did something else happen to her?

Dugan spotted his other security personnel, Buck, standing by the trees, surveying the crowd. With so many people on their normally quiet island, they were all helping and keeping an eye on things. As he approached Buck, his nervousness made him quickly get to the point. "Buck, have you seen Gina here or seen her leave?"

Buck nodded his head. "Yep. A few minutes before she arrived, I got here with a group of latecomers. I was keeping a closer eye on the bride and groom than Gina, but I did see that she wasn't here long when a man with black hair talked with her for a few minutes and they walked off down the path. I thought little of it because she seemed to know the man. Although it is rather odd she never came back after their walk."

Dugan wished Nathan had let him run full background checks on all the wedding guests. Nathan had scoffed, saying it wouldn't be necessary because all the guests were family or friends.

If Gina went with that man by choice, that was fine, but the fact that she was shirking her duties serving food for the guests and the cake was on the floor was more than enough evidence for him that everything wasn't as innocent as Buck seemed to think.

Curtly, he looked Buck in the eye and gave him strict instructions. "Something isn't right. I want you to make sure that you don't let the Riley family out of your sight. You don't have to interrupt the wedding festivities, but if one of them tries to leave, tell them I am declaring a yellow alert and they should stay put. Susan should be here any minute. Tell her I want her to do sweeps of the shoreline to make sure we don't have any unexpected visitors. I'm going to find Gina."

Dugan hurriedly walked away from the jungle, wracking his brain. Where would Gina go with one of the wedding guests? Maybe she was showing a guest around the island. He could head up to the control room and hope to glimpse her in one of the cameras, but that would only help him if she went into one of the doorways or island entry points that were under surveillance. Most of this island was just as wild as it looked.

Maybe someone needed something back at Nathan's compound and she escorted them? The thought made him feel slightly better. If a guest was sick, he could see her taking them to rest and making sure they got the care they needed, although wouldn't she have said something to Martha first if that was the case? It really wasn't like her to just take off.

A sad ache formed in his belly. He didn't even want to think about the next possibility. While he hoped that something was developing, he and Gina never actually promised each other anything. What if she had taken the guest back to her apartment? What if their kiss didn't mean as much to her as it did to him?

Dugan looked down at Suzie. "Suzie, where's Gina? Find Gina!" Suzie took off down the path, and Dugan followed. While he'd trained Suzie to find people, there were so many people here, and Gina had passed through here so many times that he was doubtful of Suzie's success.

Suzie, on the other hand, looked perfectly confident that she knew exactly where she was going. Dread continued to grow in Dugan's stomach as she led him closer and closer to the employee apartment buildings. What would he say to her if he put the entire island on alert when she had just invited a guest to have a rendezvous in her apartment?

Maybe he read into things too much and she wasn't really interested in him. Dugan knew he wasn't rich, especially handsome, or charming. What did he have to offer her? The thought felt like an ice pick stabbing into his heart. A part of him didn't want to know exactly what was going on in her apartment, but the rest of him needed to make sure she was all right. Even if it meant the end of his dreams of being with Gina.

Chapter 36

This Isn't What it Looks Like

D ugan

As he neared the employee housing, Dugan looked for Gina's window and saw the lights were all out. A small, frustrated growl rumbled from deep in his chest. She wasn't here. He should have headed to the control room. That was where he would have had the best chance of spotting her.

Suzie continued to sniff around and walked toward the front door. It was probably an old scent, but since he was already here, he checked inside, just in case. He walked upstairs to her room and rapped steadily on the door. As he expected, no one answered. He was about to walk away when he noticed Suzie nosing a crumpled-up piece of paper on the ground.

He picked up the paper and tried to flatten it as best as he could. The note only contained a handful of words, but its contents made his heart stop and his blood run cold.

Help

Trespassers

Maxwell Randolf

He recognized the handwriting as Gina's, but on this note, her handwriting was uncharacteristically a barely legible scrawl, as if jotted down in a hurry. He quickly reread the message, trying to interpret it. His Gina needed help. There were trespassers on the island. Or maybe Maxwell was a trespasser. He remembered seeing the name Maxwell Randolf on the guest list and checked him in when he arrived on his boat. The man seemed nice enough for a rich man with too much money. He even handed him a tip. Was that the man she left the wedding with?

Why would she have gone somewhere with him right before the food she made was being served? Why would she leave when her employers needed her the most? It was very unlike her. Dugan took a jagged breath and shoved the note into his pocket.

Turning and running down the stairs, Suzie padded along easily, keeping pace. Dugan's mind raced as he tried to decide where he should go next. He wished he could copy himself to cover the entire island at once. Should he waste precious time going to the control room? There were a half-dozen cameras spread out through the island, but they only covered key areas like the entrances to Nathan's compound and the dock.

The dock!

There was nowhere on the island that someone could hide for long. If anyone was trying to hurt Gina, they would try to get her away from his security team that constantly patrolled the island nowadays. While there were a few areas where someone could pull a boat ashore, they'd built the docks in Otter's Cove because it was the only place that was protected from the sea.

Suzie barked and ran ahead, and Dugan jogged behind her. "Do you smell Gina, girl? Go find Gina! She needs our help!" Soon, Suzie outpaced him and disappeared into the jungle.

Dugan pulled out his phone and called Buck. He panted as he jogged while he talked. "Hey, Buck. I need you to ask around and find out if a Maxwell Randolf is still with the other guests. Do you have anything to report?"

Buck curtly responded, "Yes, sir. I will find out if he's still here. There is nothing out of the ordinary going on here, just normal wedding festivities. I sent Susan out to check the shorelines about five minutes ago, just as you asked."

After hanging up with Buck, he dialed Susan. He didn't need to imagine copying himself when he'd trained an effective team to help him. "I need you to check the shoreline specifically for hidden boats and keep an eye out for one guest named Maxwell Randolf. I have reason to believe there are some trespassers on the island. Currently, I'm heading to the docks where I saw a Maxwell Randolf park his boat. I think he's taken Gina."

Dugan heard the bark of Pongo in the background as Susan answered. "Don't worry, sir. We will find her. I'm reaching the shore near your cottage now and will begin my sweeps.'"

Dugan said, "Thanks, Susan." He hung up and picked up his pace, but for the first time, he was truly grateful to have help on the island. He was no longer alone.

He missed his privacy, but instead of trying to do everything by himself, he had a team now. He had people he could count on not to let him down. Now he just needed to find Gina. He couldn't even let himself consider letting her down.

Dugan heard Suzie baying not too far in the distance. She must have either found Gina or cornered her prey. *Please let Gina be all right.*

Dugan came around a bend to see Suzie growling at a man with one arm around Gina's waist. Suzie had him pinned down, backed up against a ten-foot bluff. He could hear waves crashing against the rocks not far below. Gina was fighting to get loose, but Maxwell held her firmly in place. "Regina, make this dog back off so we can get out of here."

Gina kicked backward, and Maxwell grunted when she hit his shin. "Let go of me. I don't believe you for an instant, and even if I did, I would feel safer here. I'm not going anywhere."

Dugan took out a gun and stepped behind Suzie. "Let her go. Whatever you were planning, you won't get away with. Turn yourself in now, before things are worse for you."

Maxwell's eyes grew large, and he took a step backward, closer to the cliff, taking Gina with him. Gina must have realized how close she was to the edge because she stopped struggling and stayed stock-still. Maxwell scrunched up his handsome features as he frowned at Dugan. "Put that toy away and call off your mad attack dog. This isn't what it looks like. I'm trying to get my girlfriend to safety. There are some goons belonging to very rich men on their way here right now. I stopped paying their extortion after Regina left. Now that they've found her, they think they can use her to make me regret it and start paying them again."

Chapter 37

The Cost of Freedom

Gina

Gina felt Maxwell's hot breath on her neck and his strong arm secured around her waist. It made her want to be sick. At first, she tried to fight his grip, but that all changed when he took a step backward. Regardless of her feelings, she stood as still as she could. She looked down and could see the rocky drop less than a foot behind them. She didn't want to risk the fall. Suzie stood a few feet in front of them, continuing to growl, with little bits of saliva dribbling from her sharp canines.

Her heart leaped with joy when she saw Dugan enter the clearing, but she didn't know how he could get her out of this. Maxwell held her too tightly and seemed to be convinced that he was saving her by making her leave. Whatever dangers her future held, she would much rather face them here than with Maxwell.

She had agreed to leave her apartment with Maxwell because she was hoping she could make a run for it before they made it to his boat at Otter Cove. She thought she could get him trapped by one of the few snares still left on the island. Even if she could distract him for a moment, she thought she could run off and hide in the jungle until she found Dugan. She didn't stand a chance against him in her apartment, but if she got loose, he would never catch her again.

A part of her believed Maxwell was telling the truth about the extortioners coming for her. The man was egotistical enough to think he could do whatever he wanted without consequence. It was finally catching up to him, but it looked like she was about to pay the price.

Behind her, Maxwell stood awfully close to the edge of the cliff, not loosening a finger on Gina. He yelled out to Dugan, "You can back off because I'm not letting her go. I just want to keep her safe. The victim is me. I mean, I know it was stupid of me to make some money off dog fighting, but lots of people do it. I don't know why Jerry started coming after me for a share of my profits. It's not like I'm a gambling addict or anything. I did what any boyfriend would. After he started threatening to hurt my girlfriend, I hired extra security to follow her around."

Gina tried to make a fast movement to catch Maxwell unaware and break free, but Maxwell continued to hold her tight. Her voice dripped with disdain. "Why didn't you just tell me the truth instead of stifling me? Normal people don't hire bouncers to take their girlfriend shopping. I felt like I couldn't go anywhere without being followed around."

She could picture Maxwell rolling his eyes behind her as he responded, "I didn't tell you the truth because I knew you would get all high and mighty like you are right now. We were fighting about little things when this started, and I was afraid you would go straight to the cops about the dog fighting and illegal gambling. I knew you would make a big deal over a harmless past-time."

Gina could see Dugan grinding his teeth in front of her, but he kept his calm. He held up his hands, including the one with the gun, and slowly lowered it to the ground. "Listen. Whatever happened in the past is over. It sounds like we both care about Gina and don't want to see her get hurt. You can fill us in on all the details about this extortion, and I'm sure we can figure it out. I'll put down my gun, and I want you to let her go so we can all discuss this like adults."

Maxwell loosened his grip. "Move away from the gun and I'll let her go, but we still need to get out of here before Jerry's men come. I received a picture of her on this island that was taken from a boat. They ripped the picture in half as a warning. They know she's here, and I don't know what they are going to do to her. It's a lot of money they want me to pay up, and I don't intend to share another penny."

Calmly, Dugan took a few steps sideways instead of backward. His eyes never left Gina as he moved away from the gun, nearer to Gina and Maxwell. "We will take care of all of that. Gina will not get hurt, and you don't need to cave into the extortioner. I have a whole security team at my disposal trained for this very reason. We can keep her safe right here."

Before Gina knew what was happening, Maxwell pulled back his arms and released her, making her teeter on the edge of the cliff. She barely dared to breathe as she waved her arms in the empty air to keep her balance. In an acrobatic lunge, Maxwell leaped toward the gun at the same time as Suzie came barreling toward him.

Dugan threw himself forward to grab Gina's arm and pull her to safety. Maxwell caught him totally unaware as he changed direction and shoved Dugan with a shoulder to the chest, causing him to topple right over the cliff. Gina dropped to her knees and screamed as she watched Dugan fall toward the crashing waves below. He disappeared as Gina shouted, "Dugan!"

Suzie took a running leap, barked, and dove off the side of the cliff after him.

Gina watched Suzie paddle around in the water, but there was still no sign of Dugan. She stood up and turned, with a sob stuck in her throat, when she realized both Maxwell and the gun were gone. She had earned her freedom, but the cost was too great to bear.

Not caring about anything but Dugan, Gina ran beside the steep bluff, looking for an area where she could descend. She had to find him. He had to be all right.

Chapter 38

Over the Cliff

Gina

Rushing down the shoreline, Gina kept the bluffs in constant sight, trying to find any way she could descend. Not too far along, the cliff dipped down to only about six feet from a small sandy shoreline. There were enough rocky handholds that Gina risked climbing down without taking the time to fear for her own safety.

After following the bit of shoreline as far as it could go, Gina hopped from rock to rock and waded through shallow ocean water until she could see Suzie in the distance. The dog barked excitedly upon seeing her but didn't move from her spot. What would she do if something happened to the sweet man who had just risked his life for hers?

Gina got closer and saw that, in front of Suzie, Dugan lay on his back on another small sandbank, coughing. She rushed over and dropped to her knees into the shallow water beside him and leaned over the big man. After noticing a large gash on his forehead, she ran her eyes over him, inspecting him for injuries. Suzie gave a soft whine in front of her.

She took his hands in her own and looked into his eyes that were just beginning to focus on her. "Dugan! I was so worried. Are you all right?"

"Like the sun on a stormy day, I'm sure glad to see you, Gina. I should be fine, but my leg hurts like it was stuck in a bear trap. I must have hit it on a rock when I fell." Hearing him speak made her feel better inside, like everything would be okay now.

Gina bent down to look at his leg, but as she tried to pull up the hem of his pants, he groaned and got up. Gina turned and put her hands on his broad, wet chest and tried to push him back down gently. "That was a nasty fall you took. Lie still until we can get you some medical attention."

He picked up one of her hands on his chest and gave it a delicate kiss. "I'll be all right. If we go about a quarter of a mile down the shoreline, opposite from the way you came, the land evens out, and we won't have to climb the bluffs."

He sat up without moving his leg, and Suzie nosed his side until he gave her a gentle pet. He felt around in his pocket for a moment. "Do you have a cell phone on you? What happened to Maxwell?"

Gina shook her head. "No, Maxwell took my phone when I tried to hide in my bathroom at my apartment and call you. I agreed to leave with him because I thought I could get him stuck in a trap and hide in the jungle until I got help. After you rescued me, he took your gun and left. I don't know where he is now."

Dugan looked over at Gina with his brow creased in a way that sent a pang through her heart. "Gina, why didn't you tell me about him? We could have avoided all of this, or at least I could have kept a lookout for him."

Gina looked down at her hands. She hadn't meant to hurt his feelings by not telling him about Maxwell. "When I first met you, I was trying to put my past behind me, and I was having a really hard time trusting anyone after things went so sour with Maxwell. After I got to know you, I realized you would do nothing to hurt me, but I didn't want to muddy whatever was growing between us with a controlling ex-boyfriend hanging over my head. I thought I'd escaped him and was trying to move on."

Raising an eyebrow, Dugan looked at her pointedly. "Is there anything else I should know before we find Maxwell?"

Gina shrugged. "Overall, he's just rich, charismatic, and used to getting his way. I think he truly thought he was trying to keep me safe, but in the end, you must have convinced him that the island security here could do the job, or he didn't want to risk his own skin when he realized it would not be a cakewalk getting me out of here. He's gone and probably trying to get off this island right now."

Dugan grunted and hung onto the rocky cliff beside him as he tried to stand up. Gina immediately tucked herself under his free arm to help him along. He didn't complain or refuse her help, but she could tell that he was putting all of his weight on his good leg and the wall that his other hand leaned against.

They made it down the shoreline, one step at a time, until Buck saw them. With a shout, he ran over and supported most of Dugan's weight on the other side. "Sir, we were just looking for you. We apprehended one of the wedding party guests that was trying to escape with your gun and several men who tried to sneak onto the island from the shoreline. We tied them up, and Susan and Pongo are guarding them at the docks, awaiting the police. Although, it looks like we will need to call for a doctor for you too."

Dugan nodded his head. "Good work. It looks like you guys have passed your training. I'm glad to have the help."

Dugan looked over at Gina. "From one workaholic to another, how about we take a vacation?"

Chapter 39

If Not for This Pesky Leg

G ina

Suzie led the way as they walked up to the docks. Susan and Pongo stood poised in front of four men tied up to the palm tree, one of which was Maxwell. As they grew near, Pongo left his post and ran over to greet them. Dugan gave a hand signal and immediately Pongo settled down on his stomach and whined as Gina's beast master walked past. Susan called him back over, and he stood guard over the men again, this time with Suzie at his side. While still not complete, it looked like Pongo's training was going well to Gina.

Buck helped Gina to settle Dugan on a bench, and his gigantic form ended up taking up almost the whole thing. Gina sat down momentarily beside him as she helped lower him to the bench without further injuring his leg. While Dugan had his arm still wrapped around her shoulder, she moved to get up and give him his space. He gently applied enough pressure to let her know he wanted her to stay, so she did.

It was too late to do much at the wedding other than clean up. She was exhausted. The police would probably want to talk to her. Her list of excuses could keep going on and on, but deep down she knew she just didn't want to leave Dugan's side after fearing she had lost him.

It was interesting to her that nothing Dugan did ever made her feel controlled or confined. While he made his preference known that he wanted her to stay too, she knew if she tried to stand up again, he would let her go without a second thought. She could trust him.

Dugan talked to Susan. "Can I borrow your phone to update Nathan about today's events?" After Dugan finished and an alarmed Nathan was on his way, Susan called the police with an update from Dugan about the cliff incident with Maxwell and also requested a doctor. The police were already on their way, but it would be a few hours before either arrived.

***

A few hours later, a marshal came with the police, and a short while after that, a doctor arrived. The doctor was cutting Dugan's pant leg and applying a splint when the marshal untied Maxwell and took him to the side. Gina could overhear part of their discussion from where she was standing.

The marshal talked first. "Maxwell, I'm here to offer you a deal. If you testify against Jerry Marcello, we will drop your charges and put you into the Witness Protection Program..."

Gina tried to keep her eyes focused away from the two men talking so they didn't know she was listening. Maxwell scratched under his chin. "So, if I testify, I can go back to my life?"

The marshal shook his head. "No, I'm sorry. You would get a new identity and have to start all over. You can have no contact with your current life..."

The two men moved their heads closer together as they discussed details, and Gina strained her ears trying to hear. She tried to look oblivious as Maxwell walked over to her. He took her hands in his own and stared deeply into her eyes. "I agreed to go into Witness Protection, and the marshal said you can come with me. Can you imagine? We can start a new life together where I won't need to keep you under surveillance to keep you safe. Things were good between us once. We can be free. We can start a family."

Eyes opening wide in alarm, Gina stared at him silently. Over a year ago, she would have wanted nothing more than to start a family with this very man. Gina had thought she was the luckiest woman in the world that he even wanted to date her. Now, she couldn't look past the secrets, lying, gambling, and how trapped and incompetent he had made her feel.

She gently pulled her hands out of Maxwell's. She noticed Dugan was staring at the two of them intently, not paying any attention to what the doctor was doing to secure his leg. "I'm sorry, I can't go with you. I have made a life for myself here and found my family."

Maxwell hung his head. "You are a stronger woman than I ever gave you credit for. Is there anything I can say to convince you otherwise?"

She shook her head. "No, but I wish you the best of luck. I hope you find happiness in this new version of life you get to create. Don't mess it up like you did the last one."

With a small, sad half-smile, Maxwell said, "I'll try." Then he turned and walked back to the marshal. "I'm ready for my new life. Where do we start?"

Dugan limped over to Gina. "Are you all right, Gina?"

"Am I all right? You have a broken leg, and you keep insisting on hobbling around to take care of everything and everyone. Come on, let's get you inside to your rooms." Gina slid her slight frame under his right arm and wrapped an arm behind his back to help support him.

Dugan allowed himself to lean only the barest amount of his weight on her, as if glad she was there but unwilling to truly burden her. They slowly made their way to Dugan's cottage. After the door shut behind them and they were alone, Dugan quietly said, "I'm surprised you didn't go with him."

Gina, still under his shoulder, tried to look up and see his face. "Really? He hasn't been a part of my life for quite a while, and when I was with him, it was more stressful than anything else."

They reached the bed, and Dugan put one arm on Gina's shoulder to keep himself steady while he pivoted on his good leg. While sitting on his bed, he let out a low groan as she helped him lay out the injured limb. Gina moved away, but Dugan caught her hand and gave it a little squeeze. "I'm glad you stayed, but you know I can never offer you even a tenth of the things Maxwell could. I'm a simple man living a simple life."

Gina moved in closer, placing her other hand on top of Dugan's hand that held onto hers. "Dugan, you have already given me ten times what Maxwell can. You make me feel like the most treasured woman in the world. I love you."

Mouth slightly ajar, Dugan wrapped his arms around her. He said softly, "I love you too," before engulfing her in his embrace. His lips found hers, and she felt her face flush and her heartbeat quicken. She kissed him back passionately, reminiscent of their time in the caves with glittery crystals all around them. She pulled back. "Oh, Dugan. Your leg..."

Dugan let out a sensuous moan, as if it physically hurt to be parted from her. "Don't worry about my leg. Right now, I just need you." He cupped her cheeks as he lowered his head toward hers. First, his lips gently brushed against hers slowly and tenderly. She let him take the lead until she couldn't stand it anymore. Her lips tingled where he touched, and her core burned with desire. Her heart pounded as she fervently deepened the kiss, moving onto the bed beside him.

He matched her pace amorously as his heavy breathing excited her all the more. Then a groan escaped his lips that was not one born of passion. Gina pulled back, cheeks pink and lips slightly parted. "I'm so sorry! Your leg. Are you okay?"

"I'm more than okay. If it wasn't for this pesky leg..."

Chapter 40

Puppies

G ina

Two months later, Gina was humming happily as she made breakfast. Dugan came up behind her and put his arms around her waist, kissing her neck gently as she giggled. "Dugan! I'm trying to make breakfast. This isn't the time or place for this. Someone could come into the kitchen at any moment."

Her hands had a bit of egg on them from cracking a large enough batch to feed everyone, so when she turned around, she held her hands out to the sides not to get any on Dugan.

Taking advantage of her defenseless stance, Dugan wrapped his arms around her bottom, picked her up with his newly healed body, and deposited her on an empty bit of countertop. Fitting his body between her legs, he held her firmly against his strong, broad chest. Now that she was at eye level with him, she stared deeply into his blue-green eyes that looked back at her adoringly.

Her earlier gaiety was hushed by her passions as she wrapped her arms around Dugan's neck and pulled him in until their lips touched. Desire ignited in her middle as she kissed him. Her legs wrapped around his torso, pulling him against her so that every inch of the two of them touched.

"Ahem. Sorry to interrupt, but I just wanted to let you know that there is smoke coming from the oven."

Breathlessly, Gina untangled herself from Dugan to see Thomas standing in the doorway, averting his eyes. He twiddled his fingers. "I think I'll head back and whip some breakfast up for myself at my apartment today." He turned around and left.

With a groan, Gina rested her forehead on Dugan's shoulder, and he kissed the top of his head. She said, "I need to get to that," but didn't move a muscle. She could feel his heart still beating too fast, and it felt exhilarating.

"Well, I'll be a fly on the Mona Lisa. You are the most amazing woman I have ever known. I don't think I can ever go back to living without you. We can move as quickly or as slowly as you want, but I don't want to waste another moment that I could spend with you. Would you like to move into my cottage with me?"

A high-pitched screech of joy from the formal dining room interrupted them. "Yippee! Puppies!"

Dugan sighed and helped her off the countertop. "I'd better supervise Jenna picking her new companion. It's an important decision."

Gina hurried over to the oven and took out a few overly cooked rolls. Luckily, she had some pre-made pastries in the pantry she could pull out when necessary. After putting together a breakfast platter, including a turkey sandwich that the very-pregnant Brianna had requested, Gina made her way to the dining room.

Nathan and Brianna sat at the dining room table watching Jenna so intently that she didn't think they noticed their breakfast being delivered until Brianna gave her a smile and a soft thank-you. Jenna sat beside a box, letting three excited little puppies lick her hands and try to get out of the box to love her even more. "Can't I have all three? They are so cute, and I love them all."

Nathan knelt beside Jenna. "I'm sorry, Jenna, but even one puppy is going to require a lot of time and attention. Pick one, and we will let other little boys and girls have the other two to love."

Jenna frowned and gave each puppy a few minutes of attention. Eventually, she picked up the smallest of the three and snuggled her. "I'll take this one. Her name is going to be Cupcake."

Brianna called Nathan over. "Come feel. I think the baby is kicking! Mavis better get here soon to help me with this little one. Can you imagine if I delivered the baby on the island all alone?" Gina imagined herself trying to boil water, make dinner, and catch a baby simultaneously. *Whoever Mavis is, she'd better get here quickly.*

Dugan scooped up the box with the two remaining puppies, and Gina followed him into the kitchen. Gina looked into the box and the puppies tried to jump out to greet her, tails wagging wildly. "Do you have homes for these two?"

Dugan nodded. "Yeah, the big one seems like he might be pretty smart, so I'm thinking of giving him to Buck to train if he's interested. That way, we will have highly efficiently trained canine security teams ready to cover the entire island. The other one will go to a nice family that expressed interest on the mainland."

Dugan sat the box down and moved close to Gina, pulling her close and kissing her. "Now, where were we?"

Gina kissed him back and wiggled loose. "I think we moved past that part. We were about to have breakfast and you asked me a very important question."

Dugan stood stock-still, eyes focused completely on her. "Do you have an answer? I mean, we can take more time if you want to…"

"No."

Dugan's face fell, and Gina moved back toward him and snuggled into his arms. "No, I don't want to wait. I would love to move to your quiet little cottage with you."

"Gina, you have just made me happier than a fish in water. I love you." Before she could respond with more banter, he leaned down and kissed her, and she was happier than a bird in the sky.

* * *

Your Gift! Blundering Through Paradise

Download free novellas at www.mirandaherald.com

Their thirst for adventure has turned into a fight to survive...
Brothers Jackson and Nathan wanted to reconnect for the summer
on their island home. What better way than trying to impress the
women they are pining for by catching a crew of smugglers raiding
their tropical paradise?

It seemed simple enough. Set traps and let the island do the rest.
Unfortunately, unforeseen obstacles sprung up, and Jackson and
Nathan find themselves fighting for their lives. Uncovering riddles.
Deciphering clues. As Nathan and Jackson blunder through their
life-or-death adventure, they learn a little something about the greatest
mystery of all... love.

Embark on adventure in this prequel novella featuring beloved characters from ***Puzzling Through Paradise Series***.

10 Prequel Scenes from the Loves Cats Series
Excerpt from Willa's Blooper Reel

Katrina sorted all the fresh flowers into piles around her living room. *This smells wonderful. I hope they keep this powerful scent for the shower tomorrow.* She sat down in the only open space left on the floor and looked around her.

She had twenty-three flower centerpieces to finish by tomorrow. They were going to meet at eight in the morning to set up the hall for her sister, Susan's bridal shower. *I wish I had an easier time at work today. I was hoping to be fresher before tackling this.*

I'm just swamped at work right now. We had a lot of new cats come in recently. Last week, one of my volunteers told me they got a new job, and she doesn't have the time to help anymore. Another told me today that they were moving. It looks like I will be recruiting new volunteers next week.

Katrina picked up one of the glass vases and groaned. *This is going to take me all night, but what choice do I have? I guess I will have to stay up as late as it takes to finish this project.* She turned on the television in the background and filled the bottom of the vases with glass beads.

Willa sat napping behind her on the couch while she fiddled around with the flowers. Katrina tried a few different arrangements until she got the perfect look. She fiddled around with tying a perfect bow from the coordinating ribbon and then snapped a picture to send to her sister.

Good. One arrangement done, twenty-two to go. At my current rate of one flower arrangement per every half hour, that's only eleven more hours to go. Katrina put her head in her hands. *What have I gotten myself into?*

Katrina got to work. At one point, Willa came over and sat on top of a pile of flowers. "No, no, Willa. Come on. You can't sit there. You'll smash them. Here, it's almost dinnertime. Why don't I get you some food?" Katrina got up and poured cat food into Willa's dish. Willa munched happily as Katrina went back to work.

Luckily, now that she got the design down, she pumped out eight more arrangements over the next two hours. Katrina was midway through the next one when she decided that she really needed a break. She stood up, stretched her legs, and made some tea.

When she got back into the living room, she sat back down in front of her partially finished arrangement. *I thought I already put a purple one in there.* She picked up a new purple one. *I guess I didn't. The flowers are already running together.*

Katrina had twelve arrangements complete when she noticed that there were half as many of the yellow flowers as the pink and purple ones. *Oh no. The florist must have miscounted. I don't have enough yellow. What can I do? Maybe if we use the ones with yellow flowers on every other table, it won't be a big deal that some have yellow and some don't.*

She tried out arranging a centerpiece with no yellow flowers and added extra baby's breath so that they still looked full and put it beside the completed arrangements that had yellow. *I like it. Instead of being overwhelmed with yellow, it gives more of a hint of yellow.* Convinced it solved the problem, Katrina continued on.

Around two in the morning, Katrina was down to her last two arrangements. She was growing cross-eyed and developed a weird aversion to pink, purple, and yellow flowers. She reached for a flower to her side, when she realized that there were none of the pink flowers left.

Katrina became suspicious and looked around. *It's one thing if the florist miscounted the yellow flowers, but I recounted the pink and purple ones only a few hours ago. The only one other living thing in the house was... Willa.*

Katrina turned around to see Willa innocently sitting on the couch behind her. Unfortunately, the thief made a mistake. Upon closer inspection, she saw a yellow flower petal in her fur. Exhausted, she sternly asked, "Willa, what have you been doing with my flowers?"

Willa continued to look on, completely innocent. Katrina pretended like she was back at work, making another flower arrangement, while carefully watching the remaining purple flowers.

Out of the corner of her eye, she watched Willa silently pad over to the flower pile. She picked a flower up in her jaws and traveled behind the couch to sneak it out of the room, unseen. Katrina stood up slowly to see where she was taking the flower.

Willa turned the corner into her bedroom and climbed under the bed. There she laid her latest acquisition on-top of a nest of flowers she made. Immediately, she rolled all over them, crumpling the new flower to match the other ruined flowers.

Katrina felt like she could cry. *I worked so hard on these arrangements all night. I'm so close to finishing. Where am I going to get more fresh flowers at this time of night?* She gently scolded Willa for taking things that weren't hers. Willa lowered her head and slunk further under the bed, knowing she was caught.

Katrina picked up the scattered pieces of flowers. *There's no salvaging these. I simply don't have time to go pick up new flowers tomorrow morning. These last two centerpieces were for the head table. I can't just set them up there with a few purple flowers and some leftover baby's breath flowers.*

Willa looked out under the bed and softly meowed. A cranky Katrina scowled. "Maybe I should put you in one of the centerpieces. At least then it would look full. Then Susan could bring her cat, Biscuit, to put in the second one. It would look perfectly full and balanced." The offhanded comment sparked an idea in Katrina's mind.

***

The next morning, Susan gushed over the flower arrangements. "I can't believe you finished these all yourself! They turned out beautiful and smell great too."

I have an amazing opportunity for my readers. Would you like to join my community book club, have access to short stories not available anywhere else, AND read my books before everyone else?

Join my subscription community for pre-release books and exclusive exclusive content!

https://reamstories.com/page/ldxyuocbpf

A bit about Miranda Herald

Typing by moonlight and powered by tea, I love reading and writing whenever I can fit it in. I find a good mind boggling puzzle or escape room exhilarating and was excited to include them in my latest works. I hope you enjoy my puzzling twist on romance and join my characters for many more adventures!

I love to hear from my readers and want you to join my community on Facebook, Tiktok, and Instagram. Check out my website to find all of my freebies, novels, and social links. You can find everything at my website **www.mirandaherald.com.**

Join my subscription community for pre-release books and exclusive exclusive content!

https://reamstories.com/page/ldxyuocbpf